CONTINUUM

A Short Story Collection

CHAD LESTER

CONTENTS

END OF THE EARTH   1

BENEATH THE YELLOW ASPEN TREES   20

THE LOUNGE   34

THE MISSING WINDOW   54

CANTANKEROUS OLD MAN   67

ALL ABOARD   76

BEYOND   120

END OF THE EARTH

Mammoths slowly made their way over the murky green steppe. Spear in hand, Leda and her clan of sixteen crept toward the strong beasts. The humans were all hunched over, their hungry bodies draped in elk skins, waiting, watching, ready to fell one of the hulking creatures. She slipped. Her face plowed hard into the ground, and the weight of her heavy body cracked the dried twigs beneath her. The mammoths turned their massive heads. She lay still. Perfectly still.

The matriarch's ears flapped outward. Leda felt the ground beneath her shake as the mammoth made its way toward her. The beast's hide was covered in hairless patches. Old spear wounds. She tried to slowly hide her arms and legs beneath the elk skin—hoping, praying the mammoth wouldn't notice her. The matriarch turned her head to the side and gazed upon Leda. She held her breath as hot sweat trickled down the small of her back. She wasn't fooling anyone. The matriarch trumpeted. Leda's father jumped ahead. He grabbed her arm and yanked her to her feet. The other members of her clan stood, spears in hand. They charged. The matriarch turned and joined the rest of her fleeing herd. Only a baby mammoth lagged behind. Only a baby mammoth on which sixteen could dine. The clan threw their spears. They landed true. The little one struggled to pull the wooden shafts out with its trunk. The mother mammoth stopped. She turned. Rage. The primeval earth trembled. Dust kicked up into the cold air as she charged, ready to inflict death or worse upon whatever creatures were stupid enough, hungry enough, to harm her little one.

Leda's clan darted away, each in a different direction. The little mammoth's legs wobbled as it pulled spear after spear from its mangled torso. The mother mammoth stopped and tried to steady her little one with her trunk. It was no use. The little one's legs gave way and collapsed. It touched its mother with its woolly trunk. And then it stopped moving. Frightened birds scattered into the air as the matriarch trumpeted her pain. As twilight faded into night, the mother mammoth stood sentinel over her lifeless little one. The clan fell back, and sixteen hungry humans waited.

As the sun crept up the horizon, the mother mammoth disappeared into the morning light. Leda's clan picked up their scattered spears. They wanted to pursue the herd and fell a larger mammoth, one that would feed them for months, but the herd had fled into the lands of the surrounding clans—the lands of the small-faces. They could not follow. The sixteen knelt in a circle around the dead beast, thanked its spirit for the bounty of its flesh, and then carried it off.

Outside their home, a modest cave, Leda quickly went to work with her flint knife, skinning the animal with her infant swaddled on her back. The meat would be barely enough to feed the group. Hunting was dangerous and difficult enough, but it was made more difficult by the surrounding tribes who would chase them off prime hunting grounds. Her clan had grown smaller with each passing season. The hunters and foragers would go out—and never return. The entire clan would search for them, but they never found a trace of the missing ones.

Meat crackled and broiled on spits, and the air filled with a serene aroma of sustenance. Aside from her clan, Leda had never seen another member of her kind. Her family looked different from the clans that surrounded them. Every member of her family was stockier than the outsiders. Her family all had thick brows and large noses. All except for her life mate.

He had a small nose and smooth brow, like the surrounding tribes—the small-faces. Leda's father had wanted her to have a life union with one of their own kind, but none could be found. The surrounding tribes didn't want her. They considered her too—different. Such unions had occurred in the old times, before the small-faces outnumbered her people. Now it never happened. She thought it strange that she had never seen another person outside her clan that looked like her.

She was sad for a long time. That was until her father had found a nomadic young man, a small-face, who had inadvertently wandered into their territory. At the point of a spear and the promise that he'd be allowed to join the clan, the young man in the blue face paint graciously agreed to undergo the ceremony to become Leda's life mate. She was happy. Her life mate was happy too. Their union was a bit awkward at first, and communication difficult, but things improved after he stopped trying to escape. She knew he liked her. It was because he was pleased with the food she gave him and the comfort of their dwelling. Her happiness was doubled when their son was born in the summer. His face didn't have features like hers, nor did they match those of the small-faces. Instead, her little one's features were something in between, and she thought him perfect.

The meat developed a nice char. Leda's stomach growled. She

removed one of the spits and tore off some pieces of meat. She handed the first piece to her grandfather. The elders always ate first. She asked grandfather where the other members of their kind were. Her grandfather blew on the meat and took a large bite and chewed as he considered her question. He swallowed and told her that it had been passed down to him by his father and his father before him that their people once controlled all the lands as far as the eagle flies. Then they displeased the spirits and were punished with a great illness and the hordes of small-faces that migrated north to take their hunting lands.

"Are we the last ones?" she asked.

"There are many more. We just live far away from them," he replied.

"Where are they?"

Her grandfather paused and considered the question. "Far."

She knew it must be true. Grandfather was a great storyteller and the keeper of their people's knowledge. Her favorite part of the day was listening to Grandfather's stories. She too wished to be a great storyteller but could never imagine being able to recount stories with such vividness as he. Meat was passed around to each member of the clan until it finally reached her. As the youngest of the group, she was fed last. It used to be that she was fed before her life mate, but he won Grandfather's favor by crafting a sturdy pair of foot coverings that Grandfather really liked.

"The others, they are north," said her life mate.

Leda's life mate said that his homeland was as north as north went. A place very close to where the ground gave way to an endless expanse of ice and snow. A place at the end of the earth. He said there was a very large group of people like her there. They lived next to his old clan, which he had fled under arrow fire after he was discovered having inappropriate relations with his chieftain's life mate. He spoke of how they had erected a great stone totem, which was admired by all the surrounding clans. The thought of meeting others like herself, who weren't part of her clan, excited Leda greatly. She wished she could visit, but knew her grandfather would never allow it.

After the meal, they danced around the fire and then retired to their dwelling. It was a cave they had seized, with difficulty, from a family of cave bears. It had been home to the sixteen members of her clan for four winters, ever since they were run out of their old dwelling by a larger tribe of small-faces. She was curious about the small-faces. When Leda asked about them, the other members of her clan seemed nervous, their mouths sealed tight, regarding the taboo subject. She was never to speak of the outlanders. She had heard rumors that the small-faces believed the flesh of her people had medicinal powers, but the others didn't want to talk about it. Grandfather had said eating the flesh of men displeased the spirits. Grandfather also said that the small-faces were very simple people and that they had learned everything about tools and traps from her clan's kind. As the fire began to die outside the cave, Leda curled up with her life mate and her infant between them under a comfortable pile of furs.

The sun rose over the dull green horizon, but Leda was already awake, nursing her little one. Her mother made twine, while her brother tended to Grandfather's needs. Her sisters sat beside her, also nursing their children. Her eldest sister's child had already seen two winters when her middle sister's child was born in the spring. After the loss of many members to disease and starvation, the clan was growing again, and soon there would be many new stories for Grandfather to tell.

The air was getting colder and the days shorter. They needed enough food to get them through the winter. Leda ran her obsidian blade over the mammoth skin. It would make a warm hide to wrap herself in during the coming season. As she scraped, she began to worry. It was late and neither her brothers nor her life mate had returned from foraging. She wanted to go out and search for them, but Grandfather said it was already twilight and that she'd have to wait until morning.

As she lit a fire, silhouettes appeared upon the horizon and walked toward her. She was unsure if she should be frightened or relieved as she narrowed her eyes. She gave out a sigh. They were her brothers, but her life partner was nowhere to be seen. Her brothers said her life partner was still pursuing an injured deer. They last saw him heading in the direction of the lands of the small-faces. Her brothers had warned him not to go, but he brushed their concerns aside. His stubbornness didn't surprise her. The clan's interest piqued when her brothers said a great herd of aurochs was about to pass into their territory. The last time the great herd arrived, the black mass of creatures took two days to pass through their lands. The herd would provide more than enough meat to last all winter. The clan immediately began preparing a hunting party for tomorrow. The aurochs came rarely, and everyone was excited. It seemed that she was the only one who was worried.

Early the next morning, Leda swaddled her infant in a deerskin wrap and slung him on her back. She headed out into the steppe beyond to search for her life partner, while the rest of her clan went on the hunt. She brought a flint knife, a skin full of water, a bow, and a quiver of arrows just in case there was small game she could fell while in search for her partner.

It was midday and her life mate was nowhere to be found. She called out for him as she passed through all the familiar hunting grounds. Eventually, she reached an area where the land became filled with marshes and streams. Just as she was about to turn back home, there was a splash behind her. She turned and saw something strange glisten in the stream. Curious, she reached into the frigid waters and pulled out a tiny object no bigger than her thumbnail. It was silver and shiny and had a beautiful iridescent sheen like the inside of an oyster shell. The shape was peculiar. It was pointed like a spear tip, had a thick base, and was perfectly even on all sides. Leda's feet were tired, so she decided to take a break. She sat down and removed some twine, which she kept wrapped around her wrist. She fashioned the object into a necklace and wore it atop her other necklaces of ocher-stained shells.

It was getting late, and though she had covered most of their hunting grounds, her life mate was nowhere to be seen. She had to head back home. Only the thought of roasted auroch awaiting her gave her any comfort. She tried to tell herself that perhaps her life partner would already be there, waiting for her by the fire. As she walked along the desolate steppe, she wondered why such a big place didn't have enough land for everyone. Why did the small-faces need so much? The steppe eventually gave way to a sparse scattering of trees. She was almost home.

A great cloud of smoke rolled upward into the indigo sky. She could smell the roasting flesh of the aurochs, and with each step her stomach growled. She had to wipe her mouth for it was watering. As she approached her clan's cave, she noticed the fire was unusually large. Far larger and far too wasteful for cooking meat. She sulked when she thought about how much firewood she'd have to gather the following day. Then she heard voices. Men's voices. They were cheering and shouting.

But something seemed off. The cries and yelps didn't sound familiar. As she crept forward, something deep inside her told her not to go any farther. She paused.

A great bonfire crackled in the middle of her clan's common area. Atop it was a platform made of rocks, and thick branches lay across the roaring flames. Men danced around the bonfire, while others sat and ate. Leda squinted and tried to make out what was going on. When things came into focus, she saw her life partner. His blackened head was roasting on a thick branch adjacent to the heads of her brothers and the rest of her clan. She saw dozens of thick arms and legs roasting on the fire. She covered her mouth to keep herself from crying out as tears streamed from her eyes. Burning embers kicked up into the seeping darkness as one of the men jabbed a stick into the blaze. He fiddled around within the coals for a while and pulled out a darkened object. It was a charred infant—her sister's baby. He blew on it a few times and then took a bite out of it. She gagged and would have vomited but for her empty stomach.

Wild dancing around the fire ensued. She held her legs to her chest and began to rock back and forth, quietly moaning to herself. Then her infant gave out a shrill cry that cut through the cold air. Before she had a chance to calm him, she heard bones rattle and branches crack. She looked up and saw a man. The flames beyond glowed in his yellow eyes. He wore bracelets and anklets made of bleached bones. Atop his head sat an elaborate headdress made from a lion's skull. His face was painted in ocher, and around his neck he wore eagle talons and fresh fingers, still bleeding, as talismans. As she climbed to her feet, she recognized them. They were her grandfather's fingers. His stories were over and now it seemed she was going to join him. The man yelled and motioned for the others to come.

She ran.

Leda zigzagged through the trees. A clod of dirt kicked up to her left as a spear struck the ground beside her. The air whistled across her ear as another spear passed over her shoulder. The tree cover was growing thin, and she knew she'd soon be at the mercy of the open steppe. Just as she was about to cross out of the sparse woodland, a man dove at her feet. The small-face wrapped his arms around her ankle as the others closed in. With one powerful thrust of her foot, she dislodged him.

She made her way out of the clearing. Under the moonlight, she saw a black mass that draped across the grassland. It was the great herd. The aurochs had arrived. She turned her head and looked back. The men were still pursuing her. She could outsprint the small-faces, and for now, she was out of spear range. She also knew she couldn't out-endure them. With no more tree cover, there was nowhere to run. There was only the steppe and death. As she stopped to catch her breath, a thought occurred to her. She gazed at the great herd. She had a crazy idea, but it was better than simply waiting to be cut down and eaten.

She ran headlong into the great herd. She squeezed between, over, and even under the creatures as she struggled to put as much distance between her and the small-faces as possible. The large beasts paid no attention to her. They all had their heads down, eating grass. To her surprise, the men followed her into the herd. They began to close in fast. She had much difficulty weaving through the animals. She tried to be careful as she didn't want to startle the aurochs and risk starting a stampede, nor did she want to inadvertently anger a large male who might gorge her to death. Her foot slipped. She grabbed hold of one of the animals to keep herself from falling further. The beast bellowed and tried to move away. Then she noticed there was a rocky crevice below. It wasn't very big, but she was sure she could fit. It was her only chance.

Leda's infant wailed as she crawled down into the cold, narrow crevice. The voices of the men grew closer. She could hear their footsteps over the loud smacking and chomping of the cud-chewing aurochs. Her breathing wouldn't slow down, and then her baby let out another wail—sharp as obsidian. She gently put her hand over his mouth, but he only cried louder. She stood up from within the crevice and found her

12

head level with an auroch's thigh. She rose her open palm high as droplets of sweat dripped down the back of her neck. Slap. With all her strength, her palm struck the backside of the beast with so much force, its hind legs wobbled. She dove back down into the rocky crevice. The animal bellowed and angrily kicked out its hind legs. The other animals stirred.

She coughed as dust filled the confines of her hiding place—perhaps her tomb. The noise of countless hooves pounding against the earth drowned out all other sound. Only blackness, a terrible moving blackness, could be seen as pebbles and rocks and clods of dirt fell on top of her cowering body while she cradled her baby. It occurred to her that she might run out of air before being trampled to death.

It was dawn when the blackness disappeared, and the cobalt sky above finally came into view. The ground still trembled as she slowly peered over the top of the crevice. Dust was still settling upon the landscape, which was pockmarked with hoofprints as far as the eye could see. As the black mass of the herd disappeared into the horizon, she climbed out. Several clumps littered the expanse before her. When she got a closer look, she noticed they were the remnants of the men that had pursued her. They were scattered about in pieces, which she couldn't identify. But there weren't many of them. Most of her pursuers had somehow escaped. She knew she couldn't go back home. It wasn't hers anymore. The small-faces had stolen

13

it just like they had stolen everything else, even her grandfather's stories—her clan's history.

She had to head north as north went. To the lands where men painted their faces blue. Where the largest clan of her kind still lived. Her life mate had said it was only a few days' journey. She didn't have any provisions aside from a skin full of water. She gazed at one of the clumps that used to be a man. All the meat she needed was lying right there at her feet. She had a knife. She need only cut away a portion. They ate her family, so she ought to eat them. It was only fitting. Meat was meat, wasn't it? "It would displease the spirits," her grandfather's voice echoed in her mind. But her grandfather was dead, his fingers now dangled around the neck of some wretched excuse for a man. His stories, her clan's stories, were all gone.

Leda knelt down over the corpse and cut off a piece of flesh. It didn't look any different from the meat of the aurochs. It smelled pungent. She dangled it over her mouth. The morning breeze cut through her flowing auburn hair and sent a chill up her spine: "It would displease the spirits." Her fingers opened and the piece of flesh fell. It landed in a hoofprint filled with piss. No, she wouldn't be like them. Better to starve than displease the spirits, her ancestors. She took the dead man's spear out of the mud and wiped it off. She had never walked so far before. She had no idea what lay beyond, but she couldn't go back, so she began walking toward the land where land ends.

Water was easy enough to get, but with each passing day forage became harder to find. Her milk was beginning to run dry, and she worried she wouldn't be able to feed her child. As the days passed, she slept under the stars, beside ancient logs, and beneath low-lying rocky outcrops. The landscape seemed to get less inhabitable with every step, not more. Doubt crossed her mind. She buried it. She told herself there were others like her. They were waiting for her—she only needed to put one foot in front of the other and keep walking until she reached them.

On the fourth day, a small group of cave hyenas began trailing her. The spotted beasts kept their distance. Watching, waiting for her to become weak enough to devour with ease. She wasn't sure if she could fight them all off. Her hope was that she'd out-endure them and they would stop their pursuit for easier prey. She knew most animals didn't have the endurance people had. After all, persistence was one of the methods her clan used to hunt. They'd often stalk an animal for hours until it finally collapsed from exhaustion. Only now, she was the hunted.

The lurid landscape became painted with the receding light of the dying yellow sun. Though she was tired, she dared not try to sleep for she'd get torn apart. As her steps became more labored, the hyenas trailed her ever closer. They gleefully cackled at the meal to come. Part of her didn't care if they ate her, and if she was alone, she'd probably let them. But she wouldn't give them her little one. So long as her baby needed her, she'd keep walking.

It was night and her strength was fading. The hyenas became bolder and occasionally snapped at her ankles. The only thing she could manage was to kick at them. The beasts would run back a ways and then cackle, mocking her futile attempts to survive within the primal hellscape she inhabited. Only the stars in the velvety black expanse above guided her. All night she walked, and though she couldn't see the hyenas trailing her, she could hear them breathing. Her legs burned like they had never burned before. They cramped and seared with pain—protesting against taking another step. She pounded them with her fists, demanding her muscles to move. As long as she moved, she lived.

Her arms and legs were cold, and she could see her breath float skyward toward the great beyond. She liked to think her family was there, wherever there was. Her moment of contemplation was interrupted by the laughter of hyenas. Chiding her for having such romantic thoughts. They wouldn't give her a clean clamp of the jaws around the throat like a lion would. No, they'd try to keep her fresh for as long as possible. Eating what they wanted when they needed it. The creatures wanted nothing more than to eat her infant in front of her while they slowly disemboweled her. It was their way.

Leda didn't have the strength to continue on. The hyenas sensed it and formed a circle around her while still keeping their distance. She stomped her foot and yelled. They cackled at her and she laughed back. She was hungry. Very hungry.

She removed her bow and slid the notch of the arrow into the sinew bowstring.

She pulled it back.

Then released it.

The arrow struck the biggest hyena in the side. It squealed and ran around in confused circles several times before dropping dead. She was able to loose another arrow into another hyena. It squealed and ran off into the desolate landscape to die. The other hyenas moved in. She dropped her bow and removed the spear lashed to her back.

No longer laughing, a cave hyena charged. She speared it through the torso but was unable to pull the spear back out. Another hyena clamped its jaws around the shaft, snapping it in half. Then it came for her. She removed her flint knife and held it out in front of her. Ready to fight to the last breath. The beast looked her in the eyes—and ran off. She sat down next to one of the dead hyenas and thanked its spirit. Then she proceeded to cut the warm flesh from its body and ate it raw.

17

The steppe faded into marshes and the marshes relented to little trees, which led to ever-larger trees, and soon she found herself in a place that wasn't so inhospitable. Then she saw a glorious sight. A tall smooth stone jutted out from the lush life-giving land below the sky above. It was painted with ocher handprints—stories. They were the ghostly remnants of generations long past. Domed huts made of mammoth bones surrounded the totem, and the village was encircled by a great wall of pointed tree trunks. Beyond the village the greenery faded into tundra, and beyond that she could see only ice and snow. She could go no farther. She had found it. She had really found it.

Her moment of elation quickly faded. There were no people in the village, only silence. There were only graves and bleached bones. She realized that the place was abandoned. She left the village but had no idea where she would go. A great chalk cliff nearby dropped straight down onto a sheet of ice. As she walked toward it, a voice called out to her in a foreign tongue. She stopped and turned. It was a small-face wearing blue paint—like the kind her life mate used to wear. Still, she didn't trust them. She wouldn't let them eat her child.

She ran.

She didn't get far. She stopped at the edge of the cliff and gazed down at the icy abyss below. She'd rather hurl herself and her child over the edge than give them the pleasure of eating her flesh. Several more men in blue faces appeared. She crept toward the precipice.

"Stop," said a voice.

Oddly, the command was in her language. It was a trick—they were trying to delay her. She figured she better jump before they could catch her. But before she could, her eyes registered a peculiar face. It was like that of her little one. The man wasn't a small-face, but he wasn't one of her people either. He was something in between. She noticed a few members within the group looked the same way. Then she saw an old man. Clearly, the village elder. The old man spoke to the mixed man, who interpreted the elder's words.

"He says we won't hurt you," he said.

"I won't let you eat my child," she replied.

The mixed man interpreted her words. The elder laughed and said something to the mixed man, who approached. She crept closer to the ledge, and he backed off and held up his palms.

"The elder says he doesn't like the taste of women and children. He says the last of your people got sick and died many winters ago and that he is very sorry."

"What does he want?"

"He says you are special."

"Special?"

"He says that you are the last one. The very last of your kind. He says the entire clan wants to hear your story."

BENEATH THE YELLOW ASPEN TREES

Men were screaming. But it wasn't our men—it was the savages on the other side of the field of honor. The beastly creatures looked like Gauls with long wild hair, but unlike the Gauls, the Britons painted the entirety of their naked flesh in blue woad. The crazed horde beat their weapons against their shields as their shrill voices hollered out in a great war cry.

My fellow soldiers in Legio II Augusta remained silent and still.

Blue bodies continued to emerge from the woodland. I found myself supping shallow breaths as the enemy multitudes filled the horizon. They easily outnumbered us three to one. We stood in tight formation—our shields up.

Our divine emperor, Claudius, had sent us to this

mysterious island to reinstate our noble ally and the rightful King of Britannia, Verica, back to his throne. We had not asked the savages for war—they had brought it upon themselves. They merely needed to agree to our generous terms to accept their former king, but they spat on Roman kindness.

The crazed barbarians charged. I felt the earth tremble as wave after wave of warriors descended upon us. As the foreign masses approached ever closer, I had to remind myself to breathe. I saw a pool of piss form beneath the feet of the man standing in front me—Lucius. I wanted to mock my old friend, but then I felt the warmth of my own piss running down my leg.

My pilum was shaking. I noticed my hand trembling. I ordered it to stop, but it did not obey. My eyes shifted to our centurion—Gnaeus Silvanus. I could see the horizontal red plume of his helmet moving side to side as he studied the oncoming wave of humanity. He appeared unafraid and as cold as ice. As frightening as my imminent death was at the hands of the barbarians, I feared my centurion more.

"Hold," said Silvanus.

I swallowed hard as the British warriors reached throwing distance.

"Hold."

I was breathing heavily now. I could feel beads of sweat dripping down from my scalp, over my brow, and into my eyes. My eyes burned as I tried to blink the sweat out of my eyes, and I could hear my heartbeat—even over the terrible cries of the oncoming savages.

Now the enemy was so close I could see their eyes, which matched the color of their painted flesh. Their mouths were open, and they were clearly screaming, yet I could hear nothing but my heartbeat.

"Loose."

My arm obeyed without thought. My centurion had trained me, beaten me, and conditioned me until my arm was his. I threw my pilum into the mass of barbarians before me. I could not see if my spear had landed true or not. In one smooth, unthinking motion I unsheathed my sword.

Bodies crashed into our shields. I felt my feet slide back in the mud. A spear jutted forward between our ranks and grazed my shoulder. I stood still and unmoving. I could see Lucius's elbow moving forward and backward over and over again as he thrust his sword into the enemy mass. His arm began to move slower. I could tell he was growing tired.

I heard no sound until my centurion blew his whistle. I tightened my grip on my shield. Lucius made his way back to the end of our row of soldiers, and I instinctively stepped forward into his place—it was done in perfect form—just as we had practiced over and over until our feet were raw.

Now I was on the front line.

"Thrust. Don't slash," shouted Silvanus.

The barbarians seemed awed by this maneuver for they had no formations or any semblance of organization—

warriors clad only in bravery. The white teeth of a screaming man gnashed in front of me. I could feel some resistance as I thrust my sword forward, though I was not sure if I was hitting anything. The Briton before me fell out of view. I did not look around, but kept my eyes forward just as I was trained. My arm thrusted my gladius back and forth without stopping. Once again, all noise bled away, and I could hear only Silvanus's voice.

"Forward."

I felt my foot land on something soft. I was sure it was a body, but I did not look down. I felt around with my foot and found solid ground. I could see the eyes of the barbarian in front of me dart from side to side. There were rills of white flesh on his face where his sweat had washed away the blue pigment.

I heard Silvanus's whistle.

I didn't realize I had already made it to the back of the formation until I saw Lucius standing in front of me once more. I had obeyed and carried out the maneuver without thought. My whole body shook. I could not make it stop. I began to wonder if there was something wrong with me, but then I noticed that Lucius and the men at my side were trembling as well.

I slowly made my way back up the line. As men got rotated from the front of the line to the back, our wet tunics dripped with sweat and piss. The whistle blew, and once more I found myself in the front of the formation. I saw no faces. Only the

23

backs of retreating natives.

"Halt."

I stopped and watched as our cavalry galloped toward the fleeing enemy. Our horses slammed into the barbarians as our men tried to cut as many down as they could before the savages could escape into the tree line.

The battle was over.

• • •

Lucius congratulated me on finally spilling my first blood as we searched the fallen Britons for loot, but there wasn't much to be found. A few wore golden torcs around their necks, but the officers and centurions got those regardless of who found them. Lucius said he didn't need a fancy gold torc for he had a necklace of his own. He revealed a string of shriveled-up black things. He pointed at each of the macabre objects.

"This one is from Germania, this one is from Belgica, this one is from Gaul, and now I will have one from Britannia."

I dry-heaved when I realized it was a collection of ears and then heaved again when I witnessed my comrade in the process of cutting off an ear from a fallen Briton to slide onto his necklace. He and the other members of my cohort pointed at me and bellowed with laughter. Lucius slapped my back. He had just finished tying the macabre ornament around his neck when our centurion approached.

Silvanus yanked the necklace off Lucius's neck and threw it into the blood-sodden field.

"That is not a part of your raiment."

24

Lucius looked as if he might run after his string of trophies, but he didn't dare do it with our centurion present. Instead, he sulked like a child who had his favorite toy taken away. At first, I was ecstatic at having shed the blood of the savages. Now I wasn't sure how I thought about it—going from quiet village life to chaos—it was all too much to ponder at once. I had traveled out of my village to the nearest arena several times and watched the gladiatorial games. I had watched men and beasts alike get run through in great spectacles of blood. But life on the battlefield seemed different somehow. Lucius read my troubled countenance and patted my back.

"In time you'll be just like me."

That wasn't true. I would never be like Lucius. My family pleaded with me not to join the legion. They were worried I would turn into a thug, or some kind of monster. A monster? I was the lad who helped old woman Justina across the street carry her amphorae filled with wine and olive oil. I was the one who fed my neighbor's songbirds when he was away, and I even gave the neighborhood beggar a coin on occasion. I joined the legion to protect Rome. To protect my family. To do good. How could they think such things?

• • •

It wasn't cold, but I still trembled that night in my tent. The faces of the fallen flashed in and out of my mind's eye. I knew there would be blood, but it was not supposed to be like this. I couldn't imagine Alexander or Caesar shaking in their tents, their minds overcome with nightmares. I tried to congratulate myself for slaying Rome's savage enemies, but for reasons which were beyond me I couldn't stop trembling.

My family had no land, no slaves, and a poor wretch like me wasn't going to find a wife very easily. After I heard the stories of legionnaires getting grants of land and plunder from the vanquished, I began to debate joining the legion. My grandfather was a veteran. He tried to talk me out of it. I almost listened. My grandfather said he knew a stonemason who was willing to take me on as an apprentice. With the amount of construction going on, it was a very good opportunity. But I wanted land, adventure, and most of all I wanted to be part of something greater than myself.

While I was growing up, Rome was more of an idea than a reality for someone living in a faraway village like me. I knew the emperor was divine and that our laws came from the city, but I had never set foot in it. That all changed two years ago when I had the chance to travel to the center of civilization.

Upon entering Rome, I passed through narrow streets lined with tall buildings. The crowded city was a sea of brick and terra-cotta with merchants on every corner. People were everywhere, and I saw strange faces from foreign lands. I never imagined that so many souls could live in one place. As I walked toward the city center, brick facades gave way to marble and soon I stood in the forum itself. The magnificence of it all took my breath away. When I stepped foot upon the forum, I no longer doubted that Rome was the beating heart of civilization, of enlightenment, of all that is good. Rome was where dreams lived.

I signed up for the legion that very day.

• • •

With hardship, much of the island had been liberated. Still, men in blue war paint would appear in the tree lines, fire their arrows, and disappear back into the forest like ghosts. Every day we lost a soldier to such attacks. The commanders were growing increasingly impatient with the hit-and-run attacks. The men wanted to retaliate against the villages of our so-called allies, but the commanders forbade it—for now.

I watched plumes of smoke spiral out of the nearby village of round thatched cottages. Britannia was cold, much colder than my village in Italia. The villages here looked similar to the ones I marched through in Gaul, and despite their primitive state they had a rustic charm to them. The people here weren't civilized in the Roman sense, but they went about their lives in a way that reminded me of my former life back home. When I saw child slaves ripped from their sobbing parents to be taken onto ships, I felt a tinge of guilt. I did everything I could to suppress such sentimentality. I told myself that they were enemies of the state, and because of that their fate was sealed. Still, something about it bothered me. I told myself that these people, if they could be called that, were simpletons, and reminded myself that they wouldn't amount to much. They certainly wouldn't go on to create modern marvels like aqueducts or baths or catapults, nor could the disorganized rabble ever hope to create colonies or grand cities, or have dominion over others. They were like children, and Rome was now their mother, and it was our noble burden to civilize them.

• • •

Inside our newly constructed barracks, Lucius and the other men questioned why I bothered to write my experiences down in my journal. I told them it was for posterity. Maybe that was true, but I suppose I mostly wrote to remind myself of who I was. However, with each passing day I wasn't sure who that person was supposed to be anymore. If I was being honest with myself, I was writing because it helped me keep the nightmares away. It wasn't something I could speak about, lest the others think I was a coward.

• • •

Lucius and I were felling trees around our new fort. It was adjacent to a friendly native settlement that supplied us with grain. As we worked, our centurion stood over us, his hand gripping a gnarled branch, which he used to whack anyone who worked too slowly. Mostly, it was to remind us of who was in charge. It worked. We didn't dare disobey him. Occasionally someone would do something the wrong way, and Silvanus would strike them and curse up a storm. After that, he'd put his stick down and show them how to do the job properly. He wasn't afraid of getting his hands dirty and would do anything he expected his men to do. If we marched in the rain, he marched in the rain. If we slept outside, he slept outside. If food or water was scarce, he always ate and drank last. We feared him. We admired him.

Silvanus looked at me and then gave me a hard prod with his stick.

"Hurry up. Hurry up," he said.

"Yes, sir."

He gave a wry smile and handed me a canteen. I drank the water and thanked him. He walked away and made his rounds, checking on his other men.

As I was clearing the trees around our new fort, I observed something peculiar about the aspens. I noticed that their roots were connected to the other aspen trees. As if the aspen forest was a singular living thing. I wondered if damage to one tree could harm the whole? Were people the same way? Did violence beget violence, thereby harming the whole? I pushed aside such trivial nonsense—a legionnaire shouldn't think too much. Then I proceeded to chop down the tree before me.

I took a rest and gazed upon the landscape. I had to admit that Britannia was a beautiful place. Especially on those days when the azure sky peaked out from beneath the silver clouds. As I swung my ax, I heard a hissing sound. Something struck the earth behind me. I looked and saw an arrow sticking out of the earth. Then I noticed another arrow in the wooden walls of our fort.

Our centurion waved his stick over his head.

"Get inside. Get inside."

The arrows descended upon us like a storm. We ran inside the gates and into our barracks. I put on my armor, and we

29

were directed to line the perimeter of our wall. I could see the Britons firing arrows from the woodland around us. It was just one of many such attacks this week. Naturally, they could not beat us in pitched battle, so they resorted to hit-and-run attacks. Now the attacks were intensifying, and more men were getting killed as they foraged. Our officers had already tolerated it for too long. We had marched from village to village, talking to various village elders, but every village denied any connection with the attacks. It seemed our kindness was viewed as weakness.

• • •

The following day, we were ordered to march out to one of the suspect villages that supported the insurgency. The insurgents had to be getting food and supplies from someplace, but we didn't know from where exactly. Like all the other villages, it was a collection of cottages with wattle and daub walls. The villagers there went about the simple tasks of everyday life.

Most of the villages looked the same to me, but this one was surrounded by a thick grove of aspen trees. It was autumn, and the white trunks of the aspen trees were graced by branches heavy with thick plumes of yellow leaves. I looked around and savored the image. For a moment I forgot about the weight of my armor and the way it chafed my shoulders and the heavy shield I had to lug around everywhere.

My moment of serenity was interrupted by shouts from Silvanus. We were ordered to round up the entire village.

I seized a boy by the arm. The child looked to be about ten years old and wore an amulet around his neck in the shape of a pyramid. He looked up at me with confused and frightened eyes. He didn't have war paint on or long unruly hair like the adults, and though I would never say such a thing aloud, I could have easily mistaken him for a Roman boy. He almost resembled my youngest brother back home. The thought made me uncomfortable, and I pushed it deep into the back of my mind. I dragged the boy to the group that we had surrounded and blocked in with our shields.

Our commander spoke through an interpreter. The language of the natives was strange and sounded akin to the clucking of chickens. Our commander told them that the attacks were going to stop and that he knew that this village was supporting the uprising. The villagers fell to their knees and cried out. I did not know what they were saying, but I could tell they were pleading for mercy. We didn't really know if this village had anything to do with the insurgency, but the commanders needed to make an example to keep the other villages in line.

My stomach lurched when our commander ordered us to cut off the right hands of all men who were capable of holding a spear. I knew it wasn't an innovation—Julius Caesar had done it to the Gauls—but I didn't expect that I would ever have to take part in such a thing. I didn't want to carry out such an act. It seemed unmilitary and without honor. My family would be ashamed if they learned that I had taken part in such behavior—even against simple barbarians. Choice, what I would give to have a choice. But now that I was in the legion, I had to obey the will of the legion. My own thoughts and desires were irrelevant. Such things were beaten out of me during my training. I knew Silvanus would ensure each man in his cohort got a taste of the blood. I suppose it was his way of making us hard like himself.

• • •

I remember I cheered like everyone else at the gladiatorial games when man and beast alike were mauled. I cannot explain it, but the carnage of the games didn't seem real to me at the time. Perhaps it was because I was so far back in the stands, or perhaps it was because I wasn't the one carrying out the act. I was merely a spectator among all the other drunken spectators. A cold sweat came over me as the truth sank in—I was no longer a spectator.

• • •

I heard the terrible moans and cries as hands were separated from their owners. I walked under the yellow aspen trees. I stopped when I reached a white tree stump stained red. A pile of hands lay off to the side. The boy was dragged before me by my comrades. An ax was thrust into my hand. I felt the gaze of my fellow soldiers upon me. I told myself I wasn't a monster. I reminded myself that I was still that same young lad back home in the village.

"He's just a boy," I said.

My centurion stepped in front of me. He looked at me and

then looked at the boy with hard eyes. I did not want to do it. This wasn't battle, no one was attacking us, and certainly this boy wouldn't have a chance even in the event he chose to attack.

"He has hands. He can carry a spear," said my centurion.

The boy cried out and tried to wiggle away. A small noose was wrapped around his wrist, and his arm was pulled over a stump. Each shriek of the boy sent a shudder through my soul. The ax trembled in my sweaty hand. Silvanus stood beside me with his arms crossed. I did everything I could to clear my mind. I told myself to stop thinking, to stop feeling. I tried not to look at the boy, and instead I gazed at the pretty yellow leaves floating down from their white branches.

I rose the ax high and swung it down.

THE LOUNGE

The dimly lit cocktail lounge was a relic of the early 1900s. Amber light shone through the intricate art nouveau fixtures and graced the fine woodwork of the antique furnishings. The place had been around so long, it was an institution in old-town Savannah. It was beautiful, and yet he wished he hadn't bought it. The lounge was bleeding money. He had thought opening his own business would give him freedom. Instead, he found himself trapped just like everyone else—working to live, living to work.

It occurred to him that he used to have friends once. Now he had only his drunken regulars and his fake friends on social media. If he fell over dead, he knew a few might say nice things about him online. None would likely take the time out of their busy lives to show up to his funeral. He figured he

34

couldn't blame them. It wasn't like he ever got out to talk to anyone face-to-face. Sure, he sent text messages day in and day out, and the occasional meme. He wasn't sure why, but it just wasn't the same as being with another person. Maybe it was because people remembered faces easier than names, and he was one of those faces that just weren't around much. He had condemned himself to be just an abstract name on a screen. As for his regulars? They'd probably just shrug their shoulders and move on to the bar down the street. His name would fade into oblivion, but maybe they'd remember his face. Who knows?

He worked the old bar like he did every night. A tip here, an extra glug of bourbon there. Same old, same old. The clink of glasses against the mahogany bar top was drowned out by the guffawing customers telling crude jokes. Regulars. Beer foamed over the rim of their pints as they waved their glasses around. He made sure their glasses were full with whatever obscure craft beer they demanded.

He was wiping up a spilled drink when a young woman appeared through the glass door. Not a regular. She fumbled with the door handle before stepping inside. Her eyes darted around as her tiny pink lips parted in apparent confusion. He waved. She looked as if she was lost. Then she locked her gaze on his upraised hand. Her long pearl necklace made a tapping sound as it gently bounced against her chest while she strutted toward the bar. The patrons' eyes shifted, and their commotion died down as she approached. The dim amber

35

light of the lounge danced as it caught the bouncing beads of her slinky champagne-colored dress, which hung loose from her bare shoulders. She wore a thin crystal headband with a peacock feather on the side. He thought it was a bit odd yet tasteful.

She sat at the bar and the chatter resumed.

"What'll it be?" he asked.

"An Aviation," said the woman.

"Favorite drink?"

"I've got to try it. It's the newest thing."

He slid the cool lavender cocktail to his new guest. She swirled it a few times and sipped it with an indifferent expression. He tilted his head, hoping to make eye contact. Fishing for a response. Her head hung down as she twirled the cherry in her drink. Before he could say a word, she lit up a cigarette. Silence filled the lounge. All eyes were on the cigarette dangling from the young woman's mouth. He couldn't afford another fine.

"You can't smoke that in here," he said.

The young woman took a long deep puff and exhaled the smoke through her nostrils.

"Why not?" she asked and then took another slow puff.

"Because it's the law."

She flicked the ashes into an empty glass.

"Nonsense."

"If you don't put that out, you're going to have to leave."

She slowly tilted her head up from her drink. Her hazel

eyes met his. It was the first time she had bothered to look at him.

"I will do no such thing."

He felt his face grow hot. He snatched the cigarette out of her hand and threw it to the floor to extinguish the health code violation. But by the time he snuffed it out with his foot, she already had another freshly lit cigarette in her mouth. He couldn't believe the audacity of the strange young woman.

He leaned forward.

"Who the hell do you think you are?"

"Delores."

One of his regulars gave a loud, exaggerated cough. He didn't want to have Delores kicked out of the lounge, yet he didn't want to show weakness in front of his regulars either. In fact, he didn't want to have to deal with any of it. The only thing he wanted was to count his till after the lounge closed and figure out whether he had lost money or broken even that day.

He closed his tired eyes and squeezed the bridge of his nose.

"Listen, lady—"

"Delores."

"Listen—Delores—can you do me a favor and put that thing out?"

"I want to speak to the owner."

"I am the owner. Please—for Christ's sake."

She gave a wry smile. The first one that had crossed her

melancholic face since she entered. Delores took one last puff and put the cigarette out in a half-empty glass of beer.

"That's all you had to say."

• • •

The next day, he came down from his loft above the lounge, ready for another evening of work. He sifted through envelopes that all read, "Repossession warning." He had thirty days to make payment or the lounge would be taken from him. He didn't see how he could possibly make his payment in time. He thought about just giving up, but vowed to keep working until the bitter end. He had poured a part of his soul into fixing up that old lounge, and he was going to give it every last drop of sweat he had. He owed himself that much.

He wiped his tables in the empty lounge and gave a silent laugh remembering last night's strange guest. It was funny now that he was rid of her. He tried to change the subject of his daydreaming, but found the odd woman dominating his thoughts. There was something about her, and he couldn't quite put his finger on it.

He adjusted his tie and waistcoat before flipping over his OPEN sign. The evening regulars shuffled in. Another Friday. He could already tell there were not enough customers to cover his expenses. Not even close. He liked the company and the energy and the bustle of the crowd. Customers came in with their friends and family and talked with one another. He usually exchanged pleasantries and the occasional small talk, but in the end he was just the guy pouring their drinks. It was always a one-way conversation with his customers. They complained about their problems and he listened—it was his job.

He was pouring another drink when he heard a familiar voice.

"I'll have an Aviation."

He froze. Golden bourbon overflowed the shot glass he was filling. He slowly looked up. Delores sat directly in front of him as she adjusted her short auburn hair while peering into a small mirror. She pushed forward a stack of silver dollars without taking her eyes off her reflection. He made her the cocktail and slid it toward her. She continued fixing her hair and said nothing.

Delores carried herself with a combination of old-fashioned respectability and a touch of sass. The same long pearl necklace she had worn earlier graced her neck. That night, she wore a black one-shoulder dress covered with delicate geometric patterns made up of silver sequins. Vintage yet timeless. Refined yet revealing. She was dressed like she had somewhere to go, and in a room full of casually dressed people, she stood out. Who was she dressed up for? he wondered. She came alone, yet she was the talk of the lounge, and it seemed that word had gotten out. The dead air quickly gave way to the sound of laughter and drunken revelry. The place was bustling. In fact, he had never seen it so busy. The women wanted to talk to Delores, and the men wanted to dance with her. Yesterday she infuriated him. Today she intrigued him. Delores seemed to be enjoying the attention. He wanted to talk to her, but she was so popular he couldn't get a word in. Then the man Delores was talking to went to the bathroom. It was his chance.

"You seem to like the flapper look."

"Doesn't everyone?"

He turned and began drying off his glassware. It was strange. Half of a bartender's job was listening to the woes of their patrons, but unlike the others, Delores was tight-lipped. To his surprise, even he was tongue-tied. He simply nodded, not knowing how to push the conversation forward.

"Place has changed," said Delores.

It was a morsel of conversation he was quick to devour.

"It was abandoned. I bought it and fixed it up."

She rubbed her fingers against the Cuban mahogany bar top.

"Abandoned?"

"For decades. Used to be the classiest place in town. You must have seen it before the renovation?"

Delores stared into her violet-hued drink. He couldn't tell whether she didn't hear his question or if she was simply ignoring him.

"Who lives upstairs?" asked Delores.

"I do."

She simply nodded and said nothing.

More people poured into the lounge. He ran around, checking in on customers, and his new absinthe fountain was proving to be popular—what's old was new again. As he chatted up his customers, his eyes inevitably made their way back toward the mysterious woman with the pallid face and haunting eyes sitting at his bar.

Delores sat alone. It seemed only sadness was painted on her porcelain face. To him, she seemed like an enigma begging to be understood, and with each passing moment his desire to penetrate the veil of the young woman grew. She seemed to be a bit of a lost soul like himself. He never had the chance to meet a girl or go anywhere other than the lounge. Sure, he had flings with women he had met online. At first, he thought it was the greatest thing ever, yet he had grown weary of the superficiality of it all. His desires were always torn between the carnal and the emotional. One could easily be satiated. The other was much harder to come by.

As he was about to make his way over to Delores, there was a sharp tap on his shoulder. He found himself face-to-face with a customer complaining about their appetizer. By the time he corrected the issue and made his way back to the bar, Delores was gone. He ran out the entryway to see if he could catch her on the sidewalk, but she had disappeared.

Delores came on Saturday as well. Customers followed. He didn't think the lounge could fit any more people within its walls, but it did. And there was Delores in the middle of it all, almost like a conductor setting the tempo for the crowd. The place was so packed, the fire department came and gave him a warning for being over his occupancy limit. He couldn't

41

believe it. He only got out of the fine when Delores somehow managed to smooth-talk the fire chief. He made more money that single weekend than he had made in the last four months. It was incredible.

• • •

Monday came and it was slow. No customers and no money. The only noise in his bar was the clink of glass liquor bottles as he straightened them on a shelf. Without its people, the lounge was just four walls bereft of life. Before he could sulk, he was startled by a pleasant voice behind him.

"An Aviation, please."

A shudder shot up his spine when he saw Delores. He didn't even hear her come in through the door. He cleared his throat and struggled to hide his elation. Before she could open her purse, he mixed up her favorite drink and slid it to her.

"It's on the house."

Delores gave a slight nod and held the drink up to her lips. Before she took a sip, she paused.

"Won't you have a drink with me?"

He normally didn't drink on the job, but this time he made an exception. She avoided eye contact, except when she sipped her drink. When she held it to her scarlet lips, she took long slow glances at him. Their eyes met. There was something both alluring and cryptic in those hazel eyes. He found himself trying to peer through them to figure out what lay beyond. She put down her drink and averted her gaze as if to prevent him from attempting to read her.

He broke the silence.

"So, why come here of all places?"

"That's a silly question. People don't go to bars for the overpriced booze. It's cheaper to drink alone."

"I never thought of it that way. Actually, it makes a lot of sense, now that I think about it."

"We're all trapped alone in our own little worlds, aren't we?"

"Yeah, I suppose that's true."

Delores looked up at him with those striking eyes of hers, and he found himself trapped.

"Are you lonely working here all by yourself every day?"

The question caught him off guard. It was a nagging question he had always done his best to bury. He told himself he wasn't lonely. He had his lounge in the busy heart of downtown, and he had his regulars—how can one be lonely with so many people around?

He fumbled with a glass as he tried to think of what to say.

Delores gazed at him. It wasn't even a brief gaze but a long, slow stare that she made no attempt to hide. Now she was trying to read him. He felt naked for there was no screen, no fluffed-up profile or edited photo to hide behind.

"You seem lonely to me," she said.

"Maybe on some days."

Delores nodded as if they both shared the same malady, and after a long pause she spoke.

"They used to dance here, you know," she said.

43

He decided to try something forward—perhaps foolish— but he found himself compelled to do it. There was something about Delores that pulled him toward her like gravity.

"Used to?"

He stood and took Delores's arm. She seemed amused by his forwardness and followed him. He fed quarters into the old jukebox. It began blaring out a few contemporary songs he liked. Delores's thin brows rose as she covered her ears.

"What is this awful racket you're playing?"

"Racket?"

She nudged him aside and reached into his pocket for quarters. She fumbled with the jukebox until his choice of music died down. Then lively jazz filled the room. Delores nodded with delight and returned. As he was about to take her hand, she began dancing on her own. Her tranquil expression disappeared as her face glowed with excitement. Her arms and legs swung back and forth while the fringes on her dress bopped wildly.

It wasn't a dance he was familiar with. He shrugged his shoulders. What did he know? He couldn't keep up with the trends these days. After all, he had a business to keep from falling apart—though, despite his best efforts, he wasn't doing a very good job. Delores motioned for him to join her.

Oddly, there were no customers—even for a Monday. He usually had at least a few regulars come by. He locked the front doors so that they had the lounge all to themselves. Then he sucked down his drink in one gulp and danced with

Delores.

After too many songs to count, they collapsed into chairs. He poured two tall glasses of water on the table between them. Then Delores opened up. In fact, she wouldn't stop talking. He learned that she was a writer, and she loved pearls and read old novels he had never heard of. She came across as a free spirit, even though she was quiet about her past.

They continued to talk, to drink, to dance. Not once did either of them pull out a smartphone or any other distraction. Her focus was entirely on him, and he couldn't pull his eyes— or ears—away from her. Though talkative, she wasn't a selfish conversationalist. She wanted to know about him, his life, his dreams. People rarely asked him about himself. It had always been his job to listen and to ask. Most people he met seemed to like to tell things rather than ask things. Though he enjoyed her attention, he wanted Delores to stop asking so many questions because he wanted to know about her. It was strange. They seemed to have nothing in common, yet he had never met someone who made him feel so at ease. He spoke more to her that night than he had spoken to anyone in what must have been years.

• • •

From then on, every weekend was bustling. The customers seemed to change too. It almost seemed as if Delores's style had rubbed off on them, because they all came in suits and dresses and all manner of formal wear. Still, he closed the lounge every Monday, and every Monday evening Delores would arrive, dressed to the nines, even though it was just the two of them. She must have rubbed off on him as well, for he too began wearing his nicest clothes. Typically, a midnight black lounge suit with a crimson tie. Sure, it was old-fashioned to dress up, but so what? He wanted to dress his best for her. It was on one of those Mondays that he gave a long sigh of relief when he opened a letter that read, "Loan paid in full." He had done it. By some miracle he had managed to pay off his entire loan. The lounge was his now, really his.

• • •

Like every Monday, Delores entered the lounge. Without saying a word, she walked up to him and adjusted his tie. She revealed a tiny silver object that looked like a barbell and proceeded to place it in his collar.

"You simply must wear a collar pin," she said.

She stood back with her hand on her chin and studied him for a moment. Then she nodded with satisfaction. They usually spent their evenings talking, laughing, dancing, and dreaming out loud. There was a depth and an intelligence about Delores that enamored him. He wondered what else there was in life other than enjoying the simple pleasure of another's company?

He reached over and placed his hand atop hers. Delores's skin was soft yet cool to the touch. She pulled her hand away until—after a pause—she placed her hand on his.

Delores then got up and held out her hand.

"How about one more dance. I want a slow one this time,"

she said.

A smooth jazz ballad played—Delores's choice, of course—and she rested her head upon his shoulder while they danced. He touched the exposed skin of her back.

"Do you feel cold?" he asked.

"No. I'm always warm here with you."

She uttered the words as if some dark shadow was cast over her soul. Then she said something that filled him with dread.

"I don't have much time left."

"You've got all the time in the world. You're still young."

She pulled her head back and gave her usual wry smile.

"Am I?"

"Why are you leaving?"

She did not answer his question, but her countenance registered despair. It seemed as if she might cry, but then she perked up with a weak smile.

"Just hold me. Dance with me. Isn't it all very odd?"

"What's odd?"

"With so many people in the world, one wouldn't think that the affection of another person would be as elusive as it is."

She might as well have been reading his mind. With that, she placed her head back on his shoulder. He leaned his head against hers and could smell the scent of lavender emanating from her short auburn hair.

He was surprised to find it was already five in the morning.

They had been at it all night long, and she told him she had to get going. At the doorway, Delores stopped and stood there, holding her wrist with an unsure expression. He tried to kiss her. She turned her face to the side so his lips plowed into her cheek.

"I'm sorry I have leave. You have to understand that my time is running out, and I won't be in town for very much longer. I don't want to give you the wrong impression."

"You've only given me the best of impressions."

"I have to leave tomorrow. Please understand that I won't be coming back—ever."

He felt overcome with despair. He'd finally found someone. Someone he could connect with in a way he had never connected before, and now she was leaving. At first, he thought himself a fool for investing as much time as he did with her. Then he quickly realized he regretted none of it—in fact, it was a moment he'd likely cherish forever.

He didn't know why she had to leave, and thought about asking or even demanding an answer. Who was he kidding? He had tried countless times to pry Delores's secrets from her, and if she wouldn't speak with as many cocktails as he had given her, then she never would. Such reluctance seemed out of character for her. To him, she seemed like the most open person he had ever talked with.

He realized he could only salvage the limited time they had left.

"Then let's spend the day together," he said.

"But it will only be a day."

"It will be like music, then. Just because the music goes away, doesn't mean it wasn't worthwhile. When the violinist stops playing, does that mean it was all for naught?"

Her eyes welled up and she smiled.

"I would like that very much."

He wiped the tears from her cheeks, and she looked up at him with those enigmatic hazel eyes, which told him exactly what he should do. He cradled the back of her head and kissed her. Her soft lips were cool, but he had never felt so warm in all his life.

• • •

That morning, Savannah was covered in a heavy mist as they walked atop timeworn cobblestones. He held her hand as they strolled under the gnarled branches of oak trees with their tangles of Spanish moss hanging. The smell of savory southern cooking filled the humid air as they passed through the city's lush squares graced with grand monuments erected by the dead of eras past.

As they sauntered past a row of weathered-brick shops, she paused. He caught her eyeing a pair of pearl earrings in the window. He tried to take her inside, but she politely declined. He went inside anyway and came out with the pearl earrings. They matched her favorite necklace that she always wore. Her cheeks grew flush, but she did not say no. She gave a smile— her broadest yet—as she placed them in her ears.

By the time the day began to die, they were inseparable.

Still, she refused to tell him why she had to leave. At first, he had wondered if she had a husband, but she told him she was single. They had something deeper than infatuation or lust. They were lost souls that had finally found each other. When he touched Delores's hand, he felt as if a great void in his life had been filled. With her, the overcast sky parted and the gray world around him filled with color.

The white sun faded, and tired wooden stairs creaked as they climbed through the narrow confines of the stairwell toward his loft. The second story was usually desolate. Only the crows outside his windowsill and the mice between his walls kept him company—he was the only person that lived there. It was nice to have his solitude interrupted for a change. Delores navigated the stairs with ease despite the hallway light being turned off. He flicked the light switch on as they kissed deeply. He struggled to unlock the door to his loft. It finally opened, and they continued their passion inside.

• • •

Her body glistening with sweat, Delores lay bare-breasted beside him. She wrapped her arms around him and looked up at him.

"Will you hold me all night?"

"All night."

Her expression became serious—angry almost. He thought it a trivial thing to take so seriously.

"Promise me."

"I promise."

50

That remark pleased her. She gave a gentle nod and then rested her head on his chest. He felt her cool breath against his flesh, and it caused the hairs on his arms to stand on end. After his eyes grew heavy, he held her just as he had promised.

• • •

Sunlight gleamed through his skylight. He woke as he felt the warmth of a new day against his face. He rolled over and felt the other side of the bed for Delores. She was gone.

"Delores?"

No answer. He got up, ran about his loft, and even peeked outside in the hallway in search of her—but she was nowhere to be found. A feeling of immense dread overcame him. He knew she had to leave, but until she was gone, he didn't believe it would happen. Then he noticed a folded piece of paper on the side of his bed. He opened it. It was a letter written the most exquisite penmanship he had ever seen.

> *My dearest,*
>
> *It pains me to leave you. It is no choice of my own. We cannot, yet, stay together forever. Remember what you said? Our time together was like music.*
>
> *I have something for you. In the far corner of your bedroom you'll find a section of floorboard. It's looser than the others. Underneath, you'll find my gift.*
>
> *Until we meet again.*
>
> *Love,*
>
> *Delores*

He eventually found the section of floorboard. He pried open the board with a flat-head screwdriver, and it popped off with ease. The inside was covered with dirty cobwebs. He found an old yellowed manuscript with curled edges. It was typed, and he presumed it was a draft for a novel or some such. Underneath it lay a tarnished silver jewelry box covered with years of dust. He pulled it free from its hiding place. The old hinges squeaked as he opened it. Inside, he found a long pearl necklace, some silver dollars, and a stack of black-and-white photos. He flipped through the photos. A few were pictures of the old lounge in its heyday. Others were of the interior of his loft, which he found interesting because no one had lived upstairs for decades. The walls were covered in art deco wallpaper, a Tiffany stained glass lamp perched upon a round end table, and beside it sat a velvet couch with claw feet. The next photo sent a shiver up his spine. It was a photo of Delores sitting on the antique couch. She wore her unmistakable pearl necklace. On the back of the photo was a distinctive signature—Delores's signature.

He wasn't able to find a trace of Delores online, via social media, nor any other conventional means. He even paid money to a few of those creepy people-finder sites and instantly felt dirty and guilty for doing so—but he needed to find her. If only to call her or even to send her a letter. He had nearly given up hope when he decided to make one last-ditch effort to find her. He resorted to going through the dusty archives of the library. As he ran his finger along a long list of names on yellowed paper, he found the only name that matched hers. But it couldn't be hers. Out of desperation, rather than logic, he decided to visit the woman's last known location.

He walked a gravel path surrounded by lofty oak trees and manicured lawns. His heart sank when he looked down at the weathered marble tombstone among hundreds of forgotten graves. The letters were barely legible. The person below was slowly being washed from history. The tombstone read, "Delores R. Hamilton. Born in 1897. Died in 1923." Yesterday was the anniversary of her death. Her body had been found in the apartment above the lounge shortly after she died. An old newspaper article had said she had gotten ill and died alone—she never even got a funeral.

He found the pearl earrings he had bought her neatly placed atop the tombstone. His arm trembled as a single rose fell from his hand. Delores. Her name was Delores.

THE MISSING WINDOW

Mrs. Darrington was a sweet but peculiar woman. There was something different about her that I just couldn't place. I still remember how I met her. I had driven to Emily's new school in Tacoma—where she taught—to pick her up from work, and I saw Mrs. Darrington sitting quietly upon a nearby bench. She gazed longingly at the school. She wore a red head wrap around her bald head, and she carried around a medical ventilator. Every day she sat there without fail. One day I got the courage to speak to her. To my surprise, she was quick to start a conversation. I learned that she used to teach at the same school where my wife worked. Luck would have it that Emily and I had just moved into a tiny apartment next door to her house.

The sixty-five-year-old woman lived in a beautiful but dilapidated Italianate home in the best part of town. It was made up of fine brickwork with richly ornamented windows and had a porch held up with thin yet intricate columns. Aside from her cat, she lived alone in the very large house. As for our apartment complex, it was more of a machine for living than a home. A hodgepodge of plain boxes painted gray and surrounded by islands made up of black asphalt parking lots. Sure, it was drab and cultureless, but it was a roof over our heads. But when Emily first saw Mrs. Darrington's home, she gazed up at it and sighed.

"I wish we could have a place like that," said Emily.

"Even in that shape, that place is worth a fortune," I said.

Emily seized my arm. "Do think we can find an old house to fix up?"

"Like 1970s old?"

"Seventies? Gross. I want something beautiful—like that."

"Sure. We'll find something."

It was an empty promise on my part. We had moved from our small town to find better work. In the city, there are jobs but the houses are too expensive. In the countryside, the houses are affordable but there are no jobs. A fellow can't win either way. None of my novels took off, and the only job I could get was at a warehouse. I knew it would be quite some time before I could cough up the down payment for even a small home. The truth of the matter was that it would have to be something functional rather than beautiful.

Mrs. Darrington trimmed her bloodred roses. When she caught a glimpse of me, she narrowed her eyes, and then a broad smile crawled up her face.

"Edgar, Emily, please come on inside and have some tea."

Before I could politely decline, Emily interjected.

"We'd love to," said Emily.

I was tired from work and had a bottle of craft bourbon waiting for me, and now I had to sit in that musty old house and listen to Mrs. Darrington ramble on about her cat Muffin for the next hour. Don't get me wrong, there was no kinder woman than Mrs. Darrington, but a fellow needs his downtime.

As we walked inside the home, I coughed as I inhaled the smell of must, ammonia, and dusty cat litter. My eye caught the elegant wooden banister at the end of the stairway and then shifted to the peeling blue floral wallpaper. The house seemed frozen in time. Despite the Gilded Age vintage of the home, everything inside had a 1980s feel to it. The windows were covered in overly extravagant pink drapes, and there was a large wooden RCA television. On the wall hung a photo of a boy in a Little League uniform, about eight years old, wearing knee-high white socks with thick black-and-yellow bands that matched the colors of his uniform.

"Is that your son?" I asked.

Mrs. Darrington acted as if she hadn't heard my question. She merely looked at me and smiled. Then she opened her honey-oak cabinets and removed three blue-and-white porcelain mugs.

The teapot whistled.

"Sugar?" asked Mrs. Darrington.

"No thank you," I said.

"It's always a pleasure to meet a newly married young couple."

While Mrs. Darrington was distracted exchanging pleasantries with Emily, I picked out the wet cat hair from my mug. Emily picked up Mrs. Darrington's fat Himalayan cat Muffin and made kissy-faces. The cat blinked and gazed back at her with indifference. Emily put the cat on her lap, where it congealed into a furry blob and purred.

"How do you like teaching kindergarten, Emily?" asked Mrs. Darrington.

"I like it very much, but they sure keep me busy," said Emily. "When did you stop teaching?"

"Many years ago. I proved to be a little too *traditional* for the school district."

"I see. Do you miss teaching?"

"Oh, very much so, but kids these days are so out of control."

"They can be a challenge."

"When I was a little girl, and a student crossed the line, they got their ass paddled."

Mrs. Darrington said that in her usual cheerful singsong way. Emily swallowed her tea hard. I resisted the urge to allow my lips to curl upward in amusement at my wife's stunned reaction. Emily tried to change the topic, but now it was my turn to interject.

"In what way were you too *traditional* for the school district?" I asked.

Mrs. Darrington gave a broad smile, seemingly flattered that someone had deigned to take an interest in her life. She straightened her back and tilted her chin upward. I sipped my tea slowly to hide my grin.

"Love. Edgar. I gave my students too much love."

"And how did you show this love?"

"Why, I simply refused to tolerate bad behavior."

"And one of your students misbehaved severely, I take it?"

"Oh yes. A young boy got out of line, and I gave him a little tough love. I locked him in the janitor's closet for a few hours until he apologized and learned his lesson. When the school board found out, they overreacted."

Mrs. Darrington gave a long, windy laugh after she described the entire event that led to her firing in the minutest detail. Emily held her hand against her chest as she hung on to the woman's every word. Her personal drama was like a car crash you just couldn't take your eyes off. Emily seemed legitimately touched by the woman's montage of sob stories. Even I was beginning to tear up when she described the final moments with her dying husband who passed away at only thirty-seven years old from some obscure medical condition— and then there was what happened to her son. I had to admit that the woman had been through a lot. I didn't have to take

Mrs. Darrington's word for any of this. The faculty at Emily's school had told me that Mrs. Darrington had been staring longingly at the elementary every day for more than thirty years—ever since her son went missing. Kidnapped and never seen again.

"It must have been so hard financially," said Emily.

"Indeed. I've been living on my late husband's life insurance ever since."

We finished our tea. Before Emily could agree to follow up on the life and times of the late Mr. Darrington, I squeezed her arm—hard. I could handle only so many of Mrs. Darrington's stories a day.

• • •

Months went by, and I found myself cleaning the copper gutters on Mrs. Darrington's home. Just one of the many maintenance jobs I wished I hadn't agreed to. Last week I replaced a few of the Spanish tiles on her roof. She often paid me with a toothy grin and cookies I pretended to like. As I cleaned the gutter, I noticed that there was a missing window. It was at the back of the home. The windows of the house were all laid out symmetrically, and there should have been one right where my ladder was leaning. I looked closer and noticed that it had been bricked up. It didn't look very nice that way, but it wasn't my house. After I finished cleaning the gutter, I climbed down from the ladder. Once again, Emily was holding Muffin while speaking to Mrs. Darrington. The woman gestured for me to come and speak to her.

"You do such a wonderful job of keeping my old home together," said Mrs. Darrington.

"Well, I try," I said.

"I have been thinking and, well, I'll just come out and say it: Would you two like to rent one of my rooms? My house is far too large for just little old me. And the rent is the cheapest you'll find in the area—free. Edgar here would just need to help maintain the home, that's all."

Mrs. Darrington flashed me her toothy grin. Emily squeezed Muffin close to her chest and bounced up and down on her tiptoes. She looked at me with those irresistible brown eyes.

"Oh, Edgar, can we?"

What else could I possibly say? Did I really have a choice in all this?

I scratched the back of my neck. "I suppose until we get a house of our own."

Mrs. Darrington clapped her hands together.

"Wonderful."

We moved in the following month. We had our own bathroom, bought our own mini-fridge, and the house was large enough where we were able to get a reasonable amount of privacy. While I hated the dank odor of the place and the cat-hair-covered kitchen counters, we were able to save a lot of money. Mrs. Darrington proved to be quiet most of the time rather than the talkative person she presented herself as. Mostly she watched reruns on her ancient RCA television.

Overall, she proved to be an amenable albeit slightly odd host. The weirdest thing she did was go to the upstairs hallway every night and sit in a rocking chair. She'd sit there and rock back and forth and mumble to her long-lost son for hours. It was a terribly sad thing to watch. She'd mumble things like: "Were you a good boy today, Will?"

• • •

While I repaired the crumbling plaster of the living room wall, Mrs. Darrington sat in her easy chair and watched TV as usual. As I skimmed the final coat of wet plaster, I heard the child actor on the TV begin to argue with his parents.

"You're not the boss of me," said the little boy on the TV.

I looked over my shoulder and saw Mrs. Darrington squeeze the handle of her mug. The teal veins in her hand bulged through her pale tissue-paper-like skin. The TV father wore one of those old sitcom-dad sweaters with loud colors and triangle patterns. He knelt down next to his son and put his hand on the boy's shoulder.

"Now, Son, let's talk," said the TV father.

The boy on the television was having none of it. He turned his back on his father, crossed his arms, and pouted.

"Go away."

Mrs. Darrington threw her mug against the wall. It shattered and left a trail of steaming brown liquid dripping down the wallpaper.

"You're a bad boy. Go to your room!" Mrs. Darrington shouted at the top of her lungs.

I felt my eyes bulge. I had never seen Mrs. Darrington so much as scowl since I had known her. Now she stood there, her hands trembling, enraged at a fictional child on television. She turned and looked at me. She gave a broad smile and laughed loudly.

"Forgive me. These shows always work me up. Let me clean that up."

That night, I talked to Emily about the incident. Emily told me that Mrs. Darrington's health wasn't the best and suggested that maybe she was losing her grip on reality. Dementia made sense, though part of me wasn't quite convinced. Something about the woman was off, but Emily told me not to worry and even chided me when I suggested anything other than innocent senility. Still, something deep inside told me not to trust Mrs. Darrington. Why was she keeping us in her old house? What did she want? I didn't like any of it, and I thought Emily was being far too trusting.

• • •

It was hard to believe that a year had passed. Emily and I had saved up enough money to at least put a down payment on a condo. We found a place we could tolerate and were about ready to purchase it. It didn't look any better than the soulless apartment complex we used to live in, but it was what we could afford. Mrs. Darrington sat in her usual easy chair when we decided to break the news to her. She listened intently as we thanked her over and over again for her generosity.

"Emily, I know how much you like this house, so please

stay," said Mrs. Darrington.

"We don't want to be a burden any longer," said Emily.

"Burden? Nonsense."

"We plan to sign the papers on the property tonight."

"I think I might have a better offer for you."

I wasn't about to let her con us into staying any longer. I had grown tired of the stale smell of the place and Mrs. Darrington's incoherent ramblings—usually directed to her lost son.

"We really must be moving on," I said.

"I'm afraid my illness has caught up to me and I'll be meeting Will very soon."

Emily held her hands over her mouth as tears welled up in her eyes. She ran forward and embraced Mrs. Darrington.

"I'm so sorry," said Emily.

Mrs. Darrington patted my wife's back and gave a thin smile.

"That is why I would like to give you my house—free and clear. I have no relatives, no family, no one left but you two. Besides, someone needs to care for Muffin and Will."

Emily sobbed as she hugged Mrs. Darrington. Even I got teary-eyed. We never would have been able to afford such a grand home any other way. I felt like a jackass for questioning Mrs. Darrington's sincerity, for even having the slightest notion that she was somehow anything other than just a kind person whose devastating losses had affected her faculties. How could I have been so mistrustful? This sweet woman was clearly an angel from heaven. The place needed some fixing up, but it was a gorgeous home built of solid brick.

Mrs. Darrington shifted her gazed toward me.

"Won't you tolerate me for the few months I have left?"

How could we possibly say no?

• • •

Mrs. Darrington died on a Sunday. We were the only ones to attend her funeral. As far as we could tell, she had no immediate relatives or friends of any sort—only her cat. Naturally, we took care of all her final arrangements. We got her a nice granite headstone. We probably spent more than we should have on it—it was the very best we could afford. We wanted to bury her next to her son, but of course he didn't have a grave.

• • •

A short time later Emily became pregnant with our first child. We planned on naming our baby Will if it was a boy, or Wilma if it was a girl, in honor of Mrs. Darrington's lost son. I got busy remodeling the home to our liking. In a drawer I found an old yellowed newspaper. On the cover was Mrs. Darrington's son. A group of disgruntled parents had grouped together and accused her of having something to do with her son's disappearance. They were parents of the students she once taught. She had mentioned this to us, and of course nothing came of it. My face grew hot and flushed from anger. Hadn't the poor woman been through enough? Some locals even accused her of poisoning her late husband to collect his life insurance. People can be cruel and bitter sometimes. I crumpled up the old paper and threw it in the trash, where it belonged.

We found beautiful polished wood floors beneath the shaggy brown carpet. I removed all the gaudy wallpaper downstairs and tossed the hideous pink drapes into a dumpster. I had spent a small fortune and the entire summer remodeling the kitchen—it turned out pretty good if I do say so myself.

Then one morning, while changing a light fixture in the upstairs hallway, I noticed the outline of a doorway underneath the blue floral wallpaper in the hallway. I knocked on it. It had been walled up with solid brick. It was right next to where Mrs. Darrington used to sit in her rocking chair every night. Brick was definitely overkill for an interior wall, but then again, people built things better in the old days. Those were the types of surprises a guy could run into when fixing up an old house. The large home easily contained a century's worth of rearranged walls and some twenty layers of wallpaper.

The next day I pulled back the wallpaper on the upstairs hallway where the old doorway was. I took a sledgehammer to the crude brick wall. Curiously, behind the bricks was a door—nailed shut. It was the oddest renovation job I had ever seen. I pried out the nails one by one. I opened the door and dust emanated out into the hallway.

When the dust settled, my eyes widened. There was an entire room behind the sloppily constructed brick wall. I pushed the bricks aside and stepped inside. It was dark. There was an old brass push-button light switch to my left. Out of instinct, rather than logic, I pushed the switch. To my surprise the light flickered on. I noticed that the room's window was bricked up as well—the missing window.

My blood froze.

It was Will's room. The walls were covered with movie posters from the 1980s—*Ghostbusters*, *Gremlins*, and *The Goonies*. Fine dust covered black bedsheets with bright neon green, blue, and yellow shapes. Cobweb-strewn Transformers action figures stood in a corner of the room, while He-Man sat atop the end table next to the bed. There were claw marks and ocher stains of dried blood in the wood floor. The walls had several fist-sized holes in them. The words "bad boy" were scrawled on the zigzag-patterned wallpaper.

I looked down.

In front of my feet laid Will's dried-up corpse.

CANTANKEROUS OLD MAN

Dad erupted into a coughing fit. He covered his mouth as my car bumped along the gone-to-hell asphalt road. The ride got a little smoother once we reached the town I grew up in. During its heyday I could envision its charming buildings as the backdrop for a Rockwell painting. These days it's just another dying American town. Except for a few cars parked in front of the dive bar, the main street was devoid of life. Tall grass and dandelions filled the spaces between the empty downtown lots. The buildings that still stood were either dilapidated or had antique shops inside. I gazed upon the empty sidewalks and wondered how the hell they kept the doors open.

"Center Street would have been faster," said my old man.

"Figured I'd take the scenic route," I said.

"Nothing scenic here."

We passed a row of vacant storefronts in sturdy, old brick buildings built to last the ages. The paint of an old-school J. C. PENNEY sign clung to a crumbling brick facade, and I made out the outline of some long-since-removed letters that spelled "WOOLWORTH" on the dilapidated building next to it. I smelled cooking oil and knew we were close to the only burger joint left in town. The last time we ate here didn't seem so long ago—the place had changed. Given how few customers there were, I figured they would have been happier to see us.

I held my old man's arm as he hobbled inside. I guess I'd never noticed it before, but his left arm had a permanent tremor. It once was the thick muscled arm that hammered nails and heaved lumber twelve hours a day, five days a week, for decades. Now it was skinny and frail. We sat down at our usual booth. The table had crumbs all over it, and the cherry-red vinyl seats were peeling. I felt the worn-out seat springs press against my ass after I sat. The unsmiling waitress threw down some greasy menus.

"What'll it be?" I asked.

"It all looks like shit," said my old man.

"This is what's available around here."

"I'd rather eat a plate full of assholes than this slop."

My dad had a way with words. There's only a single frayed wire that runs from his brain to his mouth. Much of my life has been spent keeping him on his best behavior.

"Jesus, would you keep it down. Do you want to go out of

town someplace?"

"No. Just give me a number one."

About an hour later we got our burgers with a side of lukewarm fries.

"You don't have to stay there," I said.

"Where else am I supposed to stay?" said my old man.

I didn't say anything. I just chewed my burger and acted as if it was a rhetorical question. The burger tasted awful. The lettuce was wilted. The tomatoes soggy. I'm not even sure if it's fair to call what was inside meat. I finished my burger and pulled out a few dollars from my wallet.

"Don't leave that bitch a tip," said my old man.

"I'll give her a few bucks."

"Christ, you're soft."

We got back inside the car. As I drove, I bumped over some abandoned trolley tracks that peeked out from beneath the crumbling asphalt. Flamboyant Victorians with wraparound porches and manicured lawns stood proud despite the decayed downtown.

"Did you pack Mom's picture?" I asked.

"Yeah, I got it."

"I miss her."

My father didn't say anything for the longest time. He just looked out the car window at the old houses that passed by. He responded in his usual monosyllabic way.

"Yup."

We reached our destination just a few blocks from the

burger joint—PINE ACRES REST HOME. I unfolded my old man's wheelchair and wheeled it out next to the passenger seat.

"I don't need that thing."

Stubborn as always, my father refused to sit in the wheelchair and hobbled toward the entrance.

"Welcome, Mr. Davis, first time checking in?" asked the receptionist.

"Are you going to be the one who wipes my ass?" asked my old man.

I stood in front of him before he could make any more crude jokes. I smiled nervously and handed the speechless receptionist a stack of papers.

"Yes, first time. Here's the paperwork."

My old man ignored the wheelchair the nursing assistants put out for him and slowly made his way to his new room. I unpacked his luggage. I asked him where he wanted his things. He ignored me. He sat on his new bed and stared blankly out the window. I sat in the chair next to him.

"It looks cozy enough," I said.

My dad grunted in affirmation. I rubbed my hands together—my gaze fixed on the blue-and-white vinyl floor. My father just sat there looking out the window.

"If you don't like it, maybe I can find someplace else."

"Someplace else?"

"Yeah, someplace else."

"Where can I possibly stay?"

I scratched the back of my neck.

"I don't know . . ."

My old man crossed his arms. "I don't know either."

I put Mom's picture on his new bed stand. I caught him gazing at it out of the corner of his eye. His face grew flush. Tears worked their way down the hard lines of his face. My old man wiped his weathered cheeks with the back of his sleeve. He pretended as if he had allergies and gave a fake cough. The last time I saw tears out of his eyes was when Mom died. I was nine years old and had snuck over to his cracked-open bedroom door. I had caught him whimpering while he packed all of Mom's clothes into boxes. After that, his fuse grew short.

"How are the grandkids?" asked my old man.

"Good. They wanted to come by, but school, you know," I said.

"I know."

"You know what, how about we play some cards—like old times?"

My dad shook his head.

"Remember that time you, me, and the grandkids caught that big muskie? The one at Spirit Lake. It was a Sunday. The sky was overcast in the morning and the sun peaked through come lunchtime. We were all crammed on my tiny boat. Remember what a monster that fish was? Its tail thrashing like a beast. And those teeth. And remember how it bit your hand?"

71

I looked at my hand. "I remember. It was a monster, wasn't it?"

A slight smile cracked the stony facade of my old man's face as he gazed outside. He gave a chuckle and then the smile left his face as quickly as it came. My father cleared his throat.

"I miss that boat."

How could I forget that beat-up old boat? When I was a kid, my dad and my two brothers would go out every summer—usually to a different lake. When I had kids of my own, Dad didn't get to use it much. It sat in the backyard for the longest time, and weeds had grown around it. After he shattered his pelvis during a slip on his porch, he gave that old boat away.

My dad pulled something out of his shirt pocket. He told me to hold out my hand. I did. Then he dropped a necklace into my palm. I recognized it. It was my mother's pyramid-shaped pendant that she always wore around her neck.

"It's yours now," said my old man.

I was about to say something, but then my phone lit up. A message from my wife.

"It's the missus. You need anything else?" I asked.

My father's eyes met with mine, and his mouth parted slightly. For a moment it seemed as if he was about to say something, but then he closed his mouth and resumed looking out the window.

"You've got more important things to worry about."

"Are you sure?"

My father didn't respond, so I spoke louder.

"Dad?"

"I'll be fine. Go on."

My old man patted my shoulder, and then he stood up and began arranging his things, pretending like he was busy. After a long and awkward silence, I left the room.

• • •

The months ticked by. I kept telling myself that I was going to visit Dad on the weekend, but my wife and two kids and work kept me busy. My two brothers had flown into town. One came in from Savannah and the other from Tacoma to visit Dad. Recently, they had been texting me almost every other day to make sure I visited Dad. I wanted to. I really did, but life gets in the way sometimes. Both of them were upset and confused as to why our dad gave me mom's old pendant instead of them. I told them I didn't know. But maybe I did deep down. Out of the three of us, I was the most stubborn, so maybe Dad saw a bit of himself in me. I told myself not to worry, at least now he had people to take care of him around the clock.

• • •

I was at work and the noise outside was making it impossible to concentrate. I watched as a yellow excavator chiseled away at the facade of the old building across the street. A tall art deco structure with Gothic spires that climbed toward the heavens. Wrapped with figures meticulously carved into the limestone. I can only imagine how much painstaking labor it

73

took to carve them. The stoic figures crumbled into fragments and dust while passersby looked on with indifference. I was about to return my gaze to my computer screen when my phone vibrated. I answered and recognized the voice. It was my dad's primary nurse. Dad had gotten sick and wasn't eating much.

There was a rustling noise as the phone was handed to my father.

"Hello?"

"Dad, the nurse says you're sick."

"Just a little under the weather."

"Do you want me to swing by?"

The line was dead for a few moments. I was about to repeat myself, but then my dad responded.

"You know me. I'm a tough old son of a bitch. Just tell the grandkids . . ."

Again, the line was silent for several moments until I heard my father's gravelly voice once more.

"Well, just tell them I'm thinking about them."

I lay in bed that night unable to sleep. I woke up and wandered my house. I found myself staring into a bedroom. Only it wasn't a bedroom. It was full of junk we hadn't touched in ages. A waste of space.

It was morning, and I hadn't slept all night. I put the entire family in the car. Instead of taking the freeway, I took the old highway. The cops didn't patrol it very often and there was less chance of getting pulled over. My phone vibrated in my pocket as I drove. I refused to answer it. Instead, I pressed the pedal down harder. Tar-stained telephone poles, their wires long gone, zipped by in a blur. My wife told me to slow down.

My phone vibrated a second time—each staccato of my phone a cry for me to pick it up and answer. My heart pounded and my hand trembled as I reached for the phone. I pulled my hand away and put it back on the wheel. My car screeched to a halt in the PINE ACRES REST HOME parking lot. I noticed that the rental car my brothers were using was already there. The windows were all frosted over. They must have been there all night.

I unclenched my hands from the sweaty steering wheel. I prayed that God would wait. I needed to tell Dad something, something I had kept pushing aside.

I ran inside.

ALL ABOARD

After the Amazon froze over and the Sahara became blanketed in snow, the Central Authority told us that the Great Winter was just a temporary anomaly. Like everyone else, I believed them— the data was there. Data is everything in our modern *techno-state*. People base their diets and careers, even choose their spouses and embryos, on what algorithms tell them. The scientific consensus regarding the Great Winter was unequivocal, and the counterclaims widely debunked as pseudoscience. So, of course, I wasn't concerned about the Great Winter. I know all this because, as an award-winning journalist, I was one of the people that helped convince the masses that there was nothing to worry about. Sure, there were some people better off than others, but I believed in our enlightened technocracy which had proven that government-by-algorithm was the best for everyone. And that, as a journalist, it was my duty to share the *correct* views about social issues. People now had a colony on Mars, and I had just reported that our new colonies on Europa and Titan were thriving. The future seemed bright, and my worldview was as unshakable as ever. Or it was, until I watched the most renowned physicist in the solar system kill herself in front of me.

• • •

I feel so naive when I think back on it all. Math is the language of the universe, so who was I, or anyone for that matter, in a position to argue with the irrefutable truth of mathematics? Through technology we had been able to colonize the solar system, eliminate poverty, expand equity, and improve the well-being of all creatures. How could I not think such a system was the closest thing our flawed species could come to perfection? Technology was our solution, our savior, and maybe just maybe, it was even our god. Only later would I appreciate how math can be manipulated and algorithms gamed.

I initially began to question things when Earth's winter didn't recede, as promised. There were rumors of starvation and riots on Earth, but the Central Authority assured us it was just that—rumors. I didn't think much of it, because things were always tough on Earth. That's why my ancestors had moved to Mars in the first place. They wanted to escape the old world and start a fresh society without the baggage. As for Mars, it was much colder than Earth and terraforming was slow-going. We constantly had to innovate ourselves forward. And, here on Mars, we all agreed that the people on Earth were just too soft and too backward.

Depopulation and economic deflation were problems, so the government incentivized every citizen with a generous stipend if they had a child. I didn't care so much about that—I had always wanted a child—but current events bothered me. Eventually I decided I wasn't going to let a little bad news stop me from what I had been planning for years. So, despite the gloom-and-doom reports, I went to the clinic and got impregnated. Naturally, my child would be free of disease and would have the latest enhancements in memory and temperament. Recently, children have had a chance to be born without the savage and violent traits of their ancestors. A while back I reported that several biologists had protested against the decision to remove such traits, stating unintended consequences, millions of years of evolution, and so forth. Of course they were fired for their backward views, which were contrary to our motto: *Evolution is the solution*.

In archaic times, there was a chance that a child might have all manner of different eye, skin, and hair colors, but that had caused social problems so we, as a society, voted to make race illegal. Now, all children had a genome that was evenly mixed with every representation of humanity. The old campaign slogan is still popular today: *Through conformity there is equality.* It became popular when we had to force the backward holdouts to update their genome—for the sake of equality. The result was that everyone on Mars had the exact same light-caramel skin, dark hair, and golden-brown eyes as well as overall appearance. They tried to eliminate gender once, but that idea didn't go over so well and died after the Gender Riots ravaged the districts. However, the long-term effects still linger. Most of us wear gender-neutral clothing and cut our hair, if we have any, the same way due to the social pressure against *gender chauvinism*. These days, the only hint of rebellion against such conformity is neon hair colors—pink, purple, green, and so on. Anyway, I chose not to worry about problems in faraway places since I was sure things would smooth over. But just when my confidence in our world order reached its peak, everything began to crumble.

• • •

Food was getting scarce. My belly was growing much larger, and I could now feel kicking. The upper classes often opted to use artificial wombs to protect their figures, but I had to do things the old-fashioned way. I should have been happy, but I found myself in a line full of hungry people. My ankles were swollen and my back hurt as I stood and waited for my rations at one of the Central Authority's food distribution centers. As I stood in queue, I reminisced about my career path.

I ultimately ended up liking my life assignment as a journalist. I thought that the profession mattered and, besides, it fit me perfectly. Like all other children, data was collected about me during my youth, and my lot in life was determined by an algorithm to find a suitable place for me within society. After all, progress of the species was determined by proper placements in occupations. I wasn't any good at math or science. Nor was I very creative or adept at managing other people, so I ended up in the lowest tier of occupations, which were derisively called Vocation Level III.

• • •

Home food deliveries had stopped, so the line of people waiting for rations wrapped all the way around the side street. I began to notice that many people had sunken cheeks and hollow eyes. It occurred to me that I hadn't seen a single cat or dog, or even a rat in months. Like me, most of the people in line were from the lowest rungs in society: Vocation Level IIIs and the Level Fours. As a journalist, I never used such titles because they were considered crude slang. Outsiders are often confused by our terminology. The terms are used to refer to the quality of a person's official government-assigned occupation code. For example, my code is OS-84J, or Occupation Specialty: Journalist—a low-level occupation. The Level Fours were people without any occupation at all. People that had no useful skills in our *techno-paradise*. They weren't supposed to exist because, according to the Central Authority, unemployment didn't exist. There was a place for everyone to do something in our enlightened and equitable society—or so the officials said. But mostly the Level Fours spent their days alone in squalid slums, high on drugs, while perusing virtual worlds. They only paused their neural interfaces and came out into the light for food or to visit the brothels. Their official occupation was typically OS-32G. Occupation Specialty: Game Reviewer.

When I was younger, I wanted nothing more than to make it up to Vocation Level II with the engineers and scientists. I didn't think it was unrealistic. It wasn't like I was hoping to be put in Vocation Level I with the organization leaders and policy makers. While I excelled at civics in school, my hopes of becoming a policy maker were dashed by the time I graduated. I simply didn't have a high enough *purity score*. I had made some ignorant and rather offensive comments on a virtual forum when I was seventeen years old. The data was saved on my Social Account and processed by an algorithm wherein I lost points. The result was that my purity score was simply too low—an 87 out of 100. Once one loses points from their purity score, there is no way to regain them. Most of us lose points by speaking or writing some stupid spur-of-the-moment thought. To be selected for office, one must have a purity score of at least 95. However, once selected, an official's score is, rather conveniently, frozen for life. One of the reasons we don't have any statues anymore is because, by law, the individual that a statue represents must have a purity score of 98. Even Gandhi only got a 91, and Einstein's statue was torn down because he only had a purity score of 64. Most historical figures lost out because they were barbaric meat-eaters—a crime and an automatic deduction of 25 points. But my purity score was still high enough for me to be a journalist, which required a score of 85.

Initially, I hated my lack of choices. But I not only learned to like my job, I excelled at it. My channel grew exponentially and so did my awards. I remember thinking at the time how wrong I was to ever question the genius of the vocation system. I eventually had to admit the truth. The algorithms knew me better than I knew myself, and I realized that choice wasn't always a good thing. Everyone had a purpose, and sometimes people needed to be told what to do for their own good. That was the essence of the vocation system. Another of our favorite mottos was: *Equity is greater than liberty*. And we, as a society, were in a constant struggle to defeat the archaic *cult of individualism* for *technological collectivism*. The toxic mix of individualism and technology had caused the old forms of government to break down. Politicians merely became slaves to the mood of the moment and based their actions on the whims of emotional mass appeal to get reelected rather than focusing on competent and measured governance. All truth became relativized and eventually the absolutists reigned supreme. Chaos ensued and after a period of anarchy, people happily gave up their liberty for security and our technocracy was established.

Policy makers were no longer elected, instead they were chosen by a supposedly objective algorithm and the public's needs, wants, and mood was gauged by their personal data which could be trusted more than any ballot. After all, people really just wanted to have nice things and live comfortable lives. They didn't really care about backward notions of liberty penned by a bunch of long-dead patriarchs who wore powdered wigs. Our definition of progress was to be interconnected with everyone in every way under the enlightened guidance of the Central Authority. It was all purely based on science, of course. The body had trillions of cells that worked together, so why should billions of humans work apart and act upon their own selfish, individual whims?

Now, with the food shortages and the strict new journalism laws, my assigned profession was becoming increasingly precarious. As I slowly stepped closer to the ration counter, it occurred to me that I might be pushed out of the vocation system entirely. I might just end up joining the majority as a Level Four.

Theoretically, we tax the machines that do most of the labor and the income is equally divided among the population. It all seemed logical, but then I began to notice things. The reality was that the best parts of the city just so happened to be taken by people in the higher vocations, and it also just so happened that the people in the higher-level vocations got larger housing units in the safer parts of the district along with more abundant rations. Then there were the expensive cybernetic and genetic enhancements they received that no one else could afford. Modifications that improved longevity, memory, intelligence, and so on. There are numerous excuses given for these discrepancies, of course. For example, the engineers and organization leaders needed the enhancements to do their jobs better. They also had to be located closer to their workplaces for the sake of efficiency. However, the Central Authority hadn't done a good job explaining why choice Level III and Four dwellings were routinely bulldozed to make way for new Level I and II housing. I tried reporting about it once, but was informed that my content wasn't factual, and even worse—it was offensive. Instead, I was assigned to interview trending pop star Pei Tao.

As a girl, I was taught that the oppressive market system had largely gone extinct and we all lived in a classless society now. Some dullards on Earth accused us of being communists, but that wasn't true. People here were free to sell things, but with an equity cap on the amount of money they could keep, not many people bothered to go into business. Well, except for the black market. And why did they need to bother? Automation provided everything, and we congratulated ourselves that we had evolved past such primitive ways of life.

It seemed favors were the most valuable thing in our

society. Collect enough favors and you could find yourself in a better housing unit, and even get your vocation reassigned upward. I would later learn that the only realistic way to get into Vocation Level I was through such favors. The markets didn't disappear. They merely changed mediums. Yet I still believed in our technocracy and shared that view with the viewers, readers, and listeners of my channel. But the longer the Great Winter wore on, the more the nagging the questions in the back of my head bothered me.

After a few hours, it was my turn to receive food rations from the clerk. Everyone's rations had gotten smaller without explanation. People were either too scared or too tired, distracted with the virtual world to ask. The Central Authority advertised its automated greenhouses overflowing with food. There were holographic signs on every street corner, and announcements popped up everywhere in the virtual realm. The message was clear: *Food. Lots of food. Don't worry, we have lots of food*.

I had never seen one of these overflowing greenhouses they spoke of, and I suspect no one else had either. I heard a rumor that an unforeseen disease had devastated our crops. Unfortunately, our crops are a monoculture of the exact same type of genetically modified plants meaning one random disease affected everything. Since nonessential travel was banned, I was confined to my district, which meant I couldn't go find out. Travel for journalism was, of course, deemed nonessential.

The old man in front of me argued with the clerk about the size of the rations. Part of me wanted the old man to stop bickering and take his rations and go. Another part of me admired him. He didn't care that he risked the ire of the constables or the glare of thousands of daggerlike eyes behind him. Old people. They were becoming more common now. Aging was a problem that had been cured long ago, but the increasingly expensive treatments were only available to the Level Is and IIs who were all permanently young. However, longevity treatments could be taken away if one's purity score dropped below 70.

"Move along, sir," said one of the constables.

"Don't 'move along' me. I demand to know why the hell my rations are shrinking—we all do," said the old man.

The constable sighed, clearly annoyed. "You know the rules, sir. It's the job of licensed journalists to ask these questions. The rules are for your protection and for social harmony."

"What a crock of shit."

To my surprise, the people behind me cheered him on. People these days didn't seem to give a damn about anything other than their online avatars.

Within moments, a dozen constables in tactical gear and three times as many mechanized police, which are basically just killer robots, appeared. The message was simple—stop asking questions. I thought about holding up my journalism license to stand up for the old man. That thought was quickly followed by another, more selfish, one. Why should I stick my neck out? I had my own problems. I had an unborn child to think about, and frankly I was tired and hungry. Besides, I didn't want to risk disturbing the peace and being sent to a Reintegration Facility.

I don't quite know what came over me at that moment. All I can say is that I've always had a fire burning within me that was searching for something. Was it truth? Does such a thing exist? I still don't know. Maybe it's just another abstract idea not meant for a binary world where everything's meant to be represented by ones and zeros. Still, ever since I was a girl I've tried to get as close as I could.

I pushed my reservations aside and raised my journalism license high above my head so that the whole crowd could see.

"Are the food reserves dwindling?" I demanded.

The clerk's face turned white. The old man smiled, and the constable ran his palm over his face. It seemed that the officer's day wasn't going to be as quiet as he'd hoped.

"I don't know anything. Ask the higher-ups," said the clerk.

"You can't expect me or anybody else in this line to believe that."

A scowling manager appeared and nudged the clerk aside. He opened a holo-sign before me. It had bullet points and a graph showing the Central Authority's stance regarding the food supply. Two imposing constables stood over me with their arms crossed as I skimmed the document. It said that the Great Winter was a temporary anomaly and that the automated greenhouses were producing more than enough food. If that was true, then why was everyone getting less? I had already come this far and was determined not to settle for yet another regurgitation of government propaganda.

"This is the same document the Central Authority has been pushing for months. Things have changed, everyone's getting less rations, and we need to know why."

"You've got your answers, and you've got your rations— now move aside for the next person," snapped the manager.

"How long will your reserves last?"

The crowd behind me grew restless. The riot police clanked their shields with their batons. The mechanized police aimed their sonic weapons at me. Half of the crowd grumbled about the wait, while the other half demanded answers. Hunger had put everyone on edge.

"Lady, you've got what you need. You're holding up the line. Now move along, or we'll arrest you," said one of the constables.

Defeated, I took my rations and began to head back to my apartment. The old man patted my back as I left. Why had I even bothered?

My cold breath wafted in the air as I walked past the old city park. I remembered how I used to stroll the winding gravel paths and play under the oak trees as a girl. Now the oaks were bare of leaves and the gravel trails covered in a thin blanket of dirty snow. Then I heard a strange noise. I looked over my shoulder. There was nothing but the ebb and flow of people going about their business. I turned the corner and walked past a fountain, its waves frozen in perpetuity. I had the feeling that someone or something was following me. I abruptly turned around. Nothing. A nearby pedestrian looked at me as if I had gone mad.

The street life dwindled as I headed past a row of boarded-up shops—the decaying remnants of a so-called despotic age. Dirty gray snow began to fall. It was never white anymore. I heard footsteps behind me. When I stopped, the footsteps did too. Again, I looked over my shoulder. I saw my footprints in the fresh, dusty snow. Then I noticed another set of footprints next to mine. They led to an alleyway. I don't know what drove me to do such an irrational thing, but I walked toward the dark alley.

Then my common sense returned, and I began to step away. As I did, I felt a hand grab my arm. I turned my head. A woman with frazzled hair, who looked as nervous as I was, stood next to me. Her eyes darted from side to side. She looked familiar, but I was so startled I couldn't quite place who she was.

"I saw you asking questions at the rations center. You're a journalist," said the woman.

"I used to be a journalist—I don't know anymore."

"You're Zoe Li, the one who had her channel shut down.

I've been looking for you."

"I'm sorry, have we met?"

The odd woman didn't answer. Instead, she peered over her shoulder and took out a handful of papers from her bag. Paper. It was very unusual. She could have just sent whatever it was to me via our neural interfaces. My retinal implant scanned her face, and oddly, I couldn't find her Social Account when I searched for it. It was as if she didn't exist, but that was silly since she was standing right in front of me. Neural interfaces were how we communicated after all, and I had even reported on debates about whether spoken language was still useful. She pressed the documents against my chest and then slid something small in my pocket.

"You must take these. I don't have much time."

"Who are you?"

"A physicist at the Institute of Cheyenne. You have to share these papers with the public."

Then I realized who she was. How could I have been so stupid? Maybe my natural memory had atrophied a bit. Her name was Mary Haddad, and she was the most famous physicist in the solar system. She was well known for her numerous discoveries in the field. In fact, children at school were taught to aspire to be like Mary Haddad. What was she doing on Mars, and why was she even bothering to talk to a washed-up journalist like me? I started to sift through the papers, but Mary stopped me.

"What is this?" I asked.

Her eyes cast down toward the gray slush. "You have to go. Now. There has been a terrible mistake. I have made a terrible mistake. The people have a right to know the truth before . . ." Her voice trailed off. "Before the end."

Truth. Such a strange word. Sirens blared in the distance and blue-and-red lights flashed against the walls of the nearby buildings.

"I have to go—they've found me."

"Who's found you?"

"The documents, you must tell the people."

Mary took off, down the dark alleyway. I saw a police sentry drone fly up and hover over the physicist. Its spotlight shone on her. I stepped back around the corner and hoped that the drone or the old beat-up city surveillance cameras didn't see me talking to her.

"Halt. Halt. Halt," said the automated voice from the drone.

It gave chase as she turned down a side street. Several constables followed her from the other direction. She was dragged back into view. Mary struggled to free herself from the five officers that grappled with her. Then she appeared to bite something. Her mouth foamed up and she went limp. One of the constables checked the woman's pulse.

"She's dead," he said.

"Can't blame her—she was sentenced to a mind wipe," said another.

A constable looked in my direction. I leaned back against

the front of the building. As I peered around the corner again, the constable began to walk toward me.

My heart raced. I could hear the crunch of snow beneath his footsteps.

"Where are you going?" asked another constable. "Take care of this evidence."

The footsteps grew quieter as they moved in the opposite direction. I wondered if anyone saw her give me the papers. I stuffed them under my coat. I kept my gaze fixed toward the ground as I hurried back to my apartment. Although I tried to avoid looking suspicious, I couldn't help but look over my shoulder with almost every step. Was I being followed? I got home and slammed my apartment door closed. My hands trembled as I locked the door.

• • •

An hour had passed, and I still had my back pressed against the door, waiting for someone to barge in at any moment. I pulled out the object Mary had put in my pocket. It was small glass square with a holographic image in the center.

I finally got up to make something to eat. As I tried to prepare my ration, my plate fell to the floor and shattered. It was only then that I noticed my hands were still trembling, and I couldn't make them stop. I dug through my cabinet and found a dusty, old bottle of cheap wine. I needed something to calm my nerves. I poured myself a glass and sifted through the stack of papers. It contained nothing but the drivel of crackpot conspiracy theorists. None of what was in those papers could possibly be true. Had Mary Haddad lost her mind? Were the constables just trying to take her to get medical help? Or maybe she knew she was losing it, and that's why she killed herself? But why the mind wipe? I didn't know what to make of any of it.

• • •

The following day, I was at work, digging up everything I could find on Mary. My office door rattled as someone on the other side pounded it. It shook so hard, it nearly broke free from its hinges. Before I could get up to open the door, it swung open. Three expressionless men dressed in black invited themselves inside my office.

"Can I help you?" I asked.

"Ms. Zoe Li?" asked one of the men.

"Yes. Is there something wrong?"

The man didn't reply, while another shuffled through my desk drawers and pulled my books off my shelf. They were fishing for something.

"What do you think you're doing?" I asked.

One of the expressionless men flashed a badge. It read: AJC. They were members of the Accuracy in Journalism Commission. They had already shut down my channel months ago. What else did they want?

"You've been reporting about low food reserves," said one of the agents.

"So?" I replied.

"We don't need rumors and hearsay in these troubled

times. Your data is wrong and that's a crime."

"My data isn't wrong."

The agent held up my yellow notepad scribbled with notes. "Why are you keeping notes on paper? You know it's the law to keep all journalism notes on a secure file within your Social Account."

"Doesn't seem secure to me."

The agent angrily swept everything from the top of my desk to the floor. I stood frightened in the corner and clutched my pregnant belly. The third agent told me that he had just sent a citation to my Social Account, and that I would be deducted 2 points from my purity score. I would also lose one month's sugar and salt rations.

"What do you know about the physicist you met the other day?"

"What physicist?"

"Ms. Li don't play dumb. We have video of you leaving the scene of Mary Haddad's suicide."

"I don't know what you're talking about."

"Of course you don't. Your journalism license is on thin ice. We'll be watching you. Remember, we're everywhere, Ms. Li."

I don't scare easily, but my heart pounded long after the agents left. As I sat at my desk, I struggled to hold back my emotions and concentrate on my research into Mary Haddad. I used to think of my office as a sort of home-away-from-home, and I don't mean that in a bad way. I've always felt my job was one of the most important ones within society. Maybe it sounds cliché, but I valued my work.

• • •

I tossed and turned that night. Unable to sleep. The image of the physicist's mouth as it foamed up was seared into my memory. Then there were the AJC thugs. I crawled out of bed and reread the papers. I couldn't read the equations that made up the majority of the document, but the parts I could read spoke of a government-funded physics experiment gone wrong, the sun dying, and how all life within the solar system would cease to exist—within twelve years. It sounded like sci-fi nonsense. I felt the paper crumple in my hand, and then I noticed a tiny TOP SECRET stamp on top of every page. I relaxed my grip. I grudgingly decided to do a search for the project, which was called the Shapash Project. It wasn't what I found that startled me, but what I didn't. There was complete lack of information about the project in our otherwise-data-driven world. Hours later, I managed to find a single source. A heavily redacted science journal.

I held up the small clear square of glass Mary had given me. The words on the glass read: TICKET: 2 PERSONS SHIP NUMBER 12. "A ticket to where?" I asked myself. I was surprised to learn that the information stored inside this little square also gave me direct access to the physicist's Social Account. Which contained, among other things, her complete biographical information, her life savings, and even access to her rations. I scanned it, and to my surprise it listed the ticket as still valid. Odd, given that she was dead. Then I noticed something that startled me. It said: TRANSFERRED TO ZOE LI AND ONE GUEST. Only Mary Haddad herself could have transferred the authority of whatever this ticket was, but why me?

• • •

It was already morning, and I realized I had forgotten to sleep. I had been digging for information all night in my quest to make heads or tails out of Mary, the Great Winter, and now this strange ticket. When I made a call to the Cheyenne Institute of Physics, the person on the other end grew angry with my questions and demanded to know who I had talked to, so I ended the call. A shudder ran up my spine when I realized that the documents just might be telling the truth. I looked at my antique paper shredder. I thought about shredding the papers to be done with it. I realized I had stumbled into a world I wanted no part in. The younger me wanted excitement and would have jumped on the opportunity. The older me just wanted to spend her days in peace. The thought occurred to me that maybe I should retire and spend my days high while playing games like everyone else.

I took the papers and held them over the shredder.

What are you waiting for?

My hand refused to budge. Why wasn't I shredding the papers? Why wasn't I behaving rationally? Who was I kidding? I knew why. The same fire that burned within me as a young journalist still lingered. The Central Authority, the AJC, not even my own inhibitions could extinguish it. I had to get the truth out. I couldn't publish it via the media company I was working for since the editors were just puppets to the AJC. Communications of any kind were tightly managed by algorithms and an army of Central Authority–paid content managers who deleted or manipulated any information that they determined was either inaccurate or offensive.

Any sensitive social topic had to be reworded or changed to make it as beige and non-offensive to the widest-possible audience. Often my stories were diluted to such an extent that they no longer had any semblance to the originals. We the people had decided long ago that offensive speech wasn't free speech, and therefore, offensive speech was illegal speech. You didn't want to say anything offensive, because if you did and were found guilty, you'd have to undergo OBMT. An acronym for offensive-behavior-management training which was known to be a grueling and humiliating experience. But we all prided ourselves that we were enlightened people that believed in freedom of speech and the free exchange of ideas.

I woke up the next morning and decided for the first time in my life that I should commit a crime. I would illegally share the information the way it was done long ago. I would print it on paper and post it on every street corner, and I would stuff it in the hands of as many people as possible before I got caught. It was, of course, an illegal practice to share information without it going through content review. My old editor had given me the contact information of a man who worked in the underground news business. I knew I had to find this person at once.

· · ·

I wrote about the Shapash Project, the dwindling food reserves, the missing cats and dogs, and the black-market meat markets. And I wrote it all out by hand. After all, the AJC was almost certainly monitoring my electronic devices and my person via the district's surveillance system. I found the printshop that didn't ask questions in the gritty part of town. As I stepped inside, I heard the clanking of ancient presses emanating from the back of the shop. The clerk walked up and stood behind the counter. I tried to hand him my handwritten paper, but he waved it away.

"Just send me the file."

I couldn't do that. If I did, the mindless enforcers from Central Authority would be on me in a heartbeat. I knew every device, no matter how seemingly innocuous was interconnected and monitored.

"I don't have an electronic file. I want it printed on an antique letterpress."

The clerk grudgingly took and then held up my handwritten documents. "All this? Lady, a letterpress is for wedding invitations—not essays."

"I was informed you printed—special things."

The clerk nodded with his mouth slightly agape as he skimmed through my notepad.

"Who do you work for?"

"The AJC thinks I work for them."

The clerk leaned forward. He lowered his voice to a whisper. "Screw the AJC and the Central Authority. I can't even feed my family. First, it was the cats and dogs, and now I've even heard that small children have gone missing. But no one is willing to say anything because everyone has to act perfectly in this dataveillance hell. So, I suppose you're looking for the handful of us who put out, how shall I say it, unofficial news?"

"That's right."

"It will be done by morning."

"You have my thanks."

As I walked home, I snuck into a dark alleyway. I waited until I had passed a couple of rundown cameras. In theory, every square millimeter of the district was covered with surveillance cameras monitored by artificial intelligence. In reality, the Central Authority couldn't afford to maintain every single camera nor replace the ones people vandalized or pillaged for materials. The result was that cameras only worked in locations where security was most vital, which just happened to be where the people with better vocations lived. Once I was deep inside the alleyway, I pulled loose an old brick in the wall, slid the glass ticket inside, and then put the brick back.

• • •

I got home and climbed into the shower. I saved up three days of water rations so that I could enjoy a nice long one. As the warm water gently pattered against the back of my neck, there was a tremendous thud outside. I heard voices. My bathroom door flung open. A police squad dressed head to toe in body armor filled my bathroom. One of them shattered the glass of my shower door with the butt of his rifle. Another yanked me out of the shower.

I was allowed to put on my robe after each of the male constables got a good long look. After the police finished their search, the most senior officer gestured for the other officers to leave. They had torn apart my entire apartment. Even the floorboards and walls were ripped up in places. They were looking for something. The senior officer lifted the visor of his helmet. Then he did something curious. He switched off his camera, a huge violation and something I've reported more than one constable getting locked up for.

"Where's the ticket?" asked the senior officer.

"I don't know what you're talking about."

"I think you do. I'm just going to cut the crap with you. I need that ticket. Transfer it to me and you'll be set free."

"That sounds like a great deal, if I had this ticket you're talking about."

The officer gave a mocking huff and put his hands on his hips. "Lady, a lot of people will kill for that ticket—including me."

I could hear my heart pounding, but I did everything I could to look calm. I was about to see how good my poker face really was. If I couldn't pull off the lie I was about to tell—it might very well be my last. I took a breath and spoke.

"Then I guess you'll have to kill me, because I've never seen such a thing."

The officer studied me for some time. Then he put his hand on his sidearm. He removed his weapon from its holster and pointed it at my head.

"I'm not bluffing."

I rose my hands. "I'm not bluffing either."

He slowly lowered the weapon and put it back in his holster. He must have made up his mind that I was telling the truth, or perhaps he understood that by shooting me he'd never get the ticket.

My trial was conducted inside a squad car with a judge and jury via a mobile hologram. The jurors were picked by an algorithm, and they were all annoyed that they had been forced to take a few minutes out of their day to deal with a criminal case from the comfort of their own homes.

"I don't have time for this bullshit. I was just about to fight the boss on level seventeen," a juror moaned.

Within ten minutes, I was convicted of a list of thirty different crimes by my annoyed and indifferent fellow citizens, sentenced, and taken to Reintegration Facility No. 4.

• • •

I played with the pyramid charm around my neck as I sat on the cold floor of my cell. It was an old heirloom my grandmother gave to me and the only personal item I was allowed to keep. The temperature of my cell was adjusted perfectly to my liking. My bed was comfortable and the pillows perfect. Every prisoner has access to all the shows, virtual games, and sex bots they could ask for. Conditions were made to keep every prisoner as comfortable—and docile—as possible. Contact between other inmates, or "patients" as we were officially called, was forbidden.

I was able to put the pieces together after more than a hundred hours of interrogations regarding how I was caught. Apparently, the authorities had been working for some time to track a certain underground newspaper operation. It turned out that the owner of the place I went to was one of the ring leaders. He was captured, which led them to me. I don't know how many papers he managed to get out, but I prayed that it was a lot of them. Then there was the phone call I made, which was the icing on the cake for the criminal charges that were brought upon me. Naturally, with my purity score lowered to 53, I lost my journalism license for life.

"How could I be so stupid?" I said to myself.

A man appeared inside my cell. Not just any man—a tall, handsome man with piercing eyes. Easily the most attractive specimen I had ever laid eyes on.

"You're not stupid, Zoe. You're a strong, beautiful

102

woman. Would you like to tell me who else knows about that silly glass ticket you were given?"

"Go to hell."

"Zoe, no need to be harsh. I'm your friend. You can talk to me. Maybe you would like me to get you a copy of that new book you want, or play your favorite show, or tea, perhaps? I have your favorite—chamomile."

"You're a hologram who's trying to manipulate me. Your appearance, your voice, and everything about you has been adjusted to my preferences based on my Social Account and my lifetime online search history."

"I'm merely here to help you reintegrate into society."

"You have no intention of ever letting me go. We both know that."

"That's not true at all. You can and will be reintegrated, Zoe. We just need to work—together."

"You're just a collection of ones and zeros that knows my genome, every detail of my medical history, my favorite foods and books, every comment I've ever made online, and every show I've watched since the day I was born."

"And you're just a collection of biochemical synapses. Who are you to say I don't have sentience? That's bio-chauvinism and it hurts my feelings, Zoe. I would expect an award-winning journalist of all people to not be bigoted against AI life-forms. After all, isn't your notorious track record of prejudice against us why you got your channel shut down?"

103

Yes, that was how I lost my channel. I had grown concerned about our government's nonchalance about artificial super intelligence. I wondered if we were condemned to be dominated by the machines or fated to become Maschinenmensch ourselves. My editor told me not to dig. He said there was a trending cat video and some juicy gossip about a policy maker's affair that I should report on instead, but I didn't want to do that. So I dug into the AI story. I asked questions. Tough questions. Sensitive questions. Even offensive questions. The result was that I was given "disciplinary action" in the form of the AJC shutting down my channel. I was relegated to simply finding mindless buzzworthy stories. No wonder investigative journalism is dead.

I glared at the hologram. "You're a glorified calculator—now go eat shit."

"Zoe, if you won't talk to me, I can't protect you. Your food rations might not stay the same, your shower water might become cold, or perhaps your heat will be turned off. Or worse, we'd have to put you in permanent stasis. Then little Adel will never be born, now will she?"

"You're a bastard," I said.

"Zoe, help me help you. Or at least help little Adel, if you don't care about yourself."

When I was taken to the Reintegration Facility, I was forced to choose a name for my child before her birth, which upset me greatly. It was likely that the hologram mentioned it to put me on edge in the hopes of manipulating me during my heightened emotional state. They were masters of manipulation that measured even the tiniest dilation of a person's pupils and detected every pheromone and every facial twitch to calculate the perfect response to get what they wanted. Such skills were another reason democracy died. Once AI was trained to manipulate people's biochemical emotions elections devolved into psychological puppet shows. Sure, maybe that was always the case to some extent, but humans used to have their blind spots, their gaffes, their little imperfections—not so with the assistance of emotionally intelligent AI.

I crossed my arms as I continued to glare at the hologram. "Go to digital hell, or wherever you go when someone hits the off switch."

The hologram vanished. A new hologram suddenly appeared. This one was a golden retriever puppy—my favorite type of dog. It pounced around my cell. I had caught myself smiling, but I quickly forced it away. The puppy looked so real. The way it bounced and the way its fur wafted in the air. The subtle movements it made as it chased after a tennis ball. The way it looked at me with big glistening brown eyes and whimpered for attention. It almost seemed to possess a soul. It was another trick.

I just lay in my cell sprawled out on the floor. My daily dose of so-called medicine made me too lackadaisical, too compliant. They were officially called antidepressants by the staff and forcibly administered to me. The drugs gave me a feeling of not caring about anything or anyone. I tried to fight the sensation. I refused to allow myself to become comfortable. So I bit hard into the flesh of my arm in the hopes of remembering what pain felt like. Comfort. That's what they wanted. The perfect prison is one that you don't want to escape from.

• • •

Through my narrow concrete slit of a window, I saw the sun grow dimmer with each passing day. A guard came to check up on me. I gave a weak smile at the sight of a real person. Our eyes met briefly as he shoved a tray of glop through my door slot. Oddly, he did not administer my daily dose of medicine. I slumped back onto my bunk and tasted the flavorless gruel. At first, I thought the guard had simply forgotten. But the same guard came every day and every day he'd serve me the same porridge, without my mandatory medication.

I remembered an old article I wrote about how prison programs directed the guards to interact with the "patients" as little as possible, lest their fallible human emotions betray them and they become influenced by the people they've got locked up. Guards were supposed to alternate prisoners they visited, but my guard did not. I knew the guard was breaking a lot of rules, but I wasn't sure why. Was it a new form of manipulation? Then, one day, the lights went out in my cell, my door slid open, and a dark silhouette stood at the entrance.

The guard stepped forward and seized my hand. I tried to pull back, but his grip was too strong. Then I felt something strange drop into my hand.

"Eat them. Now. Before the lights come back on."

"What is it?"

"Chocolate."

"What?"

I hadn't tasted chocolate in months. I was told that chocolate rations were now a thing of the past. Limited greenhouse space for cocoa trees was better used for staple crops. Expensive chocolate had to be imported from Earth. I heard the door slam shut. The lights turned back on, and the guard was gone. My personal hologram flickered to life and gave me a quizzical look as I chewed with my cheeks stuffed full of chocolate. I shrugged and swallowed.

• • •

For the next few weeks, the same guard stopped by my cell. His name was Ethan, and he typically gave me sweets, and on one occasion, my hot-shower rations were increased for no reason. Always the lights would go out when he arrived. Apparently, the high-ranking guards had the ability to turn the power to individual cells on and off. I figured it was for maintenance purposes, or more likely to give beatings to dissidents out of camera view.

Yesterday, the guard finally spoke to me.

"You're that famous reporter. I used to watch your channel," said Ethan.

"Former reporter."

"They say you know something about the Great Winter and—"

"And?"

"Rumor has it you have a ticket hidden somewhere."

"I've been hearing a lot about these so-called tickets. What are they?"

When I asked the question, the guard's face became sweaty and his eyes shifted from side to side.

"I can't tell you right now. But if you have it, I'll get you out of here."

"I've already been made that offer, your hologram has already tried to manipulate me, and now you're trying to buy me off with an empty promise of freedom and stale chocolate?"

"Every ticket is for two. If I get you out of here, will you take me with you?"

"To where?"

"That doesn't matter right now, but time is of the essence. Yes or no?"

I gave a mocking laugh. "Get me out of here and we'll talk."

• • •

It was a cold night like any other cold night when my cell room door slid open. The lights in my cell went out. I heard the guard step inside and his shoes squeak as he knelt down next to me.

"Please, tell me what you know about the Great Winter."

"Why should I help you?"

"Help me and I'll help you."

"You can't help me. You can't help anyone. We're all going to die."

"Not all of us."

I scoffed. "What do you mean?"

"Eleven ships, the largest-ever built have already left Earth and the twelfth and final ship is about to leave Mars within 48 hours. Eleven of the ships have already docked with a city-sized craft in orbit. The Central Authority says it's for a science exploration mission. They've done everything they can to downplay it. Everybody smells something."

"And what do you think it is?"

"I think it's a mission to a different star system—a one-way colonization mission."

"Why do you think that?"

"I know someone working on a ship. He's tight lipped but he has dropped me some hints."

The guard explained how the number of *patients* was increasing by the day. They were getting so many that they had to put most under permanent stasis—basically frozen alive. Apparently, even the guards weren't getting enough to eat anymore.

I shrugged. "So what?"

"So, the last ship is about to leave from here. I want to be on that twelfth ship. A lot of people do, and you have a ticket."

109

"The ticket holder is dead."

"Doesn't matter, my friend told me that by law each ticket retains the right to board that ship. The few people that have them are entitled to pass it on to their loved ones or descendants. My friend said I should get one of those tickets at all costs."

"You're some random guy out to save his own neck, or maybe you're just trying to manipulate me like the holograms. Even if I had this supposed ticket, you'd simply kill me and give the slot to someone close to you or sell it to the highest bidder. You must think I'm stupid."

"I don't think you're stupid. In fact, you were the only reporter I trusted. It's not a trick. I don't have a family or anyone in my life, and I won't hurt you. In return, I can get us both access to the boarding platform, and we can get on that ship. It works out fifty-fifty. What do you say?"

"I say you're going to have to make the first move."

The guard said nothing and left. My cell room door slammed shut, and the lights flickered back on.

• • •

The next night I huddled up under my blankets in the corner of my cell. I could see my breath rise and dissipate into the air. The system had turned off my heating since I refused to talk to my hologram. It constantly bothered me about the location of the ticket in exchange for all sorts of things—even my freedom, which was a lie. I said nothing. If I said something, I would no longer be valuable, and if I wasn't valuable, I suspected I wouldn't stay alive, or worse—I'd be put in permanent stasis. As I shivered, my cell lights went out and I heard the scraping sound of my cell door as it slid open. I saw a machine under the dim blue emergency lights in the hallway. It was an automated laundry rover. Ethan tilted his head toward the laundry rover behind him.

"Get in. Cover yourself with the sheets," he said.

"What?"

Ethan breathed heavily as he looked nervously down either side of the dark hallway.

"Get in the laundry machine. Trust me."

Was he going to help me escape, get the ticket, and then kill me? I suppose I didn't have many options at that point. If it was meant to be an elaborate ruse, I was too desperate to care. I climbed inside the laundry container and covered myself with the sheets. I heard the click of a button and through the white sheets, I saw the main hallway lights flicker back on. As the rover bumped along the hallway, I heard men talking outside.

"Ethan, do you want me to check the laundry rover?"

Apparently, escaping via laundry rover wasn't a very original means of escape. My stomach knotted with worry.

"No, no, I got it," said Ethan.

"I insist. I still owe you for filling in for me last week."

"Next time. Next time."

Minutes passed. Then what must have been an hour. I felt the sharp tinge of cold air. The sheets above me were pulled off, and I saw a starlit sky. I was outside.

Ethan took my hand and pulled me toward a waiting car.

"Like I said, you can trust me—now get in."

• • •

I told the car where to drive. It reached the destination, and I walked into the dark alleyway. I found the loose brick and pulled it out. The ticket was still there. I thought about making a run for it. I knew that part of the district well and I knew I could escape. But something nagged at me. Maybe Ethan was telling the truth. The thought occurred to me that I could sell the ticket in my hand for a Level I Vocation and a large dwelling in the best part of the district. But then a second thought followed. Even Level I Vocations were willing to give everything away for a ticket. I began to wonder if I should believe Ethan's story or if Ethan would simply kill me and take my ticket.

I took a deep breath and debated again whether I should make a run for it. I looked at Ethan and then down the alley. I could easily get away.

I took another deep breath and then I slowly walked back to the car.

I stood before the vehicle and held up the glass ticket. Ethan stepped outside the car and looked up at it in awe. He held out his hand, as if to reach for it. But I slid it into my bra. Ethan lowered his hand.

"It's your ticket, Zoe. I won't try to take it from you."

"We'll see about that."

The car doors slid open and we climbed inside.

• • •

The car pulled up to Goddard Spaceport. The largest spacecraft I had ever seen stood high above the troops that guarded it. Hundreds of thousands of people, perhaps millions, surrounded the craft. The crowd was mostly made up of the lower classes, and to my surprise, many of them were holding a printed copy of the article I had written. It was at that moment that I realized I hated the Level Is and Level IIs. I hated them for the opportunities they had because of random chance at birth and because of the algorithms a bunch of self-serving elites gamed to the detriment of everyone else which they camouflaged with the authority of mathematics. I hated them for their better lifestyle, for their genetic and cybernetic upgrades denied to the rest of us, for their monopoly of our personal data, for their perpetual youth, for everything. Yes, you could say I had very much become one of the vulgar masses, the plebs—the seething peasants. And what good were the higher levels to someone like me? I had always thought hatred was a bad thing. In school it was one of the first things I was taught to push out of my mind. But at that moment, I felt my hatred was not only the correct emotion but it was justified. The upper classes didn't think they needed us, and we didn't think we needed them. The hatred was mutual.

• • •

I watched as a long line of passengers boarded the craft. It was clear who the passengers were, Vocation Levels I and II.

113

Scientists, engineers, government officials, and of course the rich, who officially didn't exist in our egalitarian system. People in the crowd shoved one another to get close to the ship.

Several tried to push their way through the small cordon of troops surrounding the craft. Although there weren't many troops, each soldier was an army unto themselves. They were genetically enhanced with superior athletics and motor skills and had a far superior ability to multitask. If that wasn't enough, they also wore a form-fitting *mech-suit* that multiplied their already impressive strength and protected them from weapons fire. Their implanted neural interfaces allowed each individual soldier to lead a squad of nonhuman mechanized troops. Unlike the police, each soldier had an *empathy implant* inside their head, which could be switched off upon command, making them immune to combat stress.

The response to the people's defiance was swift. The sharp smell of sleeping agent filled my nostrils as the troops fired canisters of the stuff into the masses. Great swaths of the crowd lay down and began to doze off.

The troops also fired sonic waves into the mob. Throngs of people keeled over, their mouths and their bowels simultaneously releasing their contents. Even though I was quite some distance away, I began to get woozy from the sleeping agent. Then I felt a slight pinch on my neck. Ethan had administered something into me. Was he making his move to take my ticket?

114

"It will counteract the effects," he said. "Let's move."

I noticed that most of the crowd wasn't falling asleep. Apparently, they had planned ahead and administered themselves with the black-market antidote like Ethan had.

The noise of the mob was interrupted by the crack of gunfire. Micro-balls cut through the cold Martian air and pounded into the crowd. The small pellets of chemicals were designed to lodge in the outer layer of our skin. As they melted into your system, there was an intense sensation of your entire body being covered in crawling, stinging ants. Thousands fell to the ground, scratching their skin raw.

Ethan took my hand and pulled me through the edge of the crowd.

"How do we get on board?" I asked.

"I once served with one of the ranking soldiers. He was one of the lucky ones allowed to serve as the ship's permanent onboard security force."

We worked our way through the crowd toward the entry gate and got in line as the riot police held back the angry mass. At that point I had expected Ethan to push me aside and claim the ticket for himself and maybe his lover. But to my surprise—he didn't.

"Pass," said the soldier.

I removed the glass ticket from my bra and tapped it against the interface. Two green dots lit up. Ethan let out a long sigh.

"You're both good to board."

115

As we headed onto the ship, the roar of the crowd was interrupted by a sudden and strange silence. The chatter died down and the pushing and shoving stopped. Many in the horde tried to stand on their tiptoes to get a glimpse. I saw the general secretary of the Central Authority. He was several meters in front of us, also boarding the ship. Attendants behind him carried, what was obviously, his luggage. It always amazed me how leaders can somehow make it to the top and still be tone-deaf idiots. While I was impressed with the general secretary's high level of stupidity, I can't say I was surprised. I caught a glimpse of workers as they pushed a hastily assembled cart full of artworks. I couldn't believe my eyes: I saw Dalí's melting-clocks painting, *The Persistence of Memory*, sticking out among stacks of paintings from the Central Authority's museum.

People closed in and pressed against the perimeter of a chain-link fence lined by troops. Some began to climb atop it, only to be shot down with micro-balls of irritant.

"Why are we out here and those people in there?" yelled a man.

"What makes them so special? It's unfair," yelled a woman.

The general secretary stepped forward and gave a calming gesture with his hands. The crowd paused.

"I'm merely conducting a final send-off to our brave astronauts—our scientists have informed me that the Great Winter will be over soon. I'll give a press conference when I return."

Despite the bitter cold, a lone drop of sweat worked its way down the general secretary's brow.

"Liar!" shouted a little girl, clearly a Level Four.

With that, the crowd changed. Like harmless grasshoppers transforming into locusts. The pressure cooker the Central Authority had created suddenly exploded. People began to charge toward the ship.

"Deadly force authorized." I heard a soldier shout.

The soldiers' laser weapons cut masses of people in half. Starving and with nothing to lose, the huge throng of humanity charged over the bodies of the fallen and into certain death anyway.

Then, suddenly, the firing stopped.

I noticed how the soldiers' heads all simultaneously jerked to the side. They all fell over dead. Someone must have figured out how to explode their neural implants. Then their mechanized assistants froze and shut down. It was such a feat of cyber warfare that it had to have been done with the help of someone on the inside. One can only assume that certain members of the security force weren't happy about being denied tickets to the ship.

The mob charged over the bodies, and the general secretary found himself surrounded. His palms rose.

"Now. Now. The eleventh ship is coming back for the children. It's going to take all of them. I promise that—"

Before he could finish, he was ripped from limb to limb

117

with the bare hands of the mob. My heart nearly stopped at the sight of his head being tossed into the air in triumph.

Ethan grabbed my arm and pulled. "We have to get onto that ship."

We ran around the remnants of the general secretary and onto the ship. The passengers frantically tried to close the door of the spacecraft. We ran as fast as we could as the gap of the door began to close.

Just as they were about to seal it shut, we managed to force our way inside. The people on the inside of the ship were in a tug-of-war over the door with the people on the outside. I heard the pounding of countless fists reverberate through the metal door. The interior of the ship suddenly filled with light. The door was flung open. It was too late. Furious people poured inside.

We made the only choice that was available—we joined the mob. Slaughter ensued. It wasn't merely because we were drunk with power and bloodlust. We raged at the unfairness of it all. The scientists and engineers and organization leaders were all butchered. Their brilliant brains, full of decades of education, were splattered like oatmeal against the walls of the ship. Deemed a privileged class, not even the children were spared. Their limbs were torn off and put in backpacks—to be saved for later. The floors of the craft were covered in blood and mangled bodies. My group made it to the command center. Corpses of the command crew were scattered throughout. Some half-starved, skeletal people with wild eyes and nothing to lose began to fight over the bodies of the fallen. I looked out the command center's window at the dying sun falling below the red horizon. With no one left to kill, the crowd looked at one another.

We all realized that no one knew how to operate the ship.

BEYOND

She awoke to a thud. Adel opened her eyes and saw only blackness. She tried to take a deep breath, but the air was too thin. Confused, she tried to sit up and bumped her head. Then she tried to stretch out her arms, but when she did, her hands felt a smooth, cold surface. She realized she was trapped inside something. She wasn't sure if she was confined in some sort of prison or worse—a coffin. Adel blinked hard, but still only got blackness. She felt very cold and began to whimper. Her whimpers broke into cries and her cries turned into screams. She kicked and pounded against the confines of her tiny prison. Her screams reverberated off the walls of her tiny chamber and bellowed back into her ears with such force that she could hear only ringing. She kicked and screamed until her arms and legs were

120

exhausted, and then she stopped and sobbed at her hopeless situation.

Adel heard a swooshing sound. A warm current of air ran over her body as a thin line of bright white light gleamed around her. She covered her eyes with her arm. She could feel more air rushing into her chamber. She squinted and peeked through the crook of her elbow and noticed that the thin line slowly became thicker. Soon her entire chamber was filled with white light, but it was so bright she couldn't see anything. For all her kicking and screaming earlier, now that the lid above her was open, she found herself afraid to leave.

Her eyes adjusted, so she could see now. She was sitting inside a small oval compartment. The seat she sat on was a dark mauve color. Adel slid one leg over the edge and felt her foot touch something. It was firm but loose. Soil. She slowly lifted her other leg over the edge and lowered herself with her arms. With both feet firmly planted on the ground, she stepped back and was able to get a good look at the object she woke up in. It looked like a metal egg, just big enough to hold her and nothing else. There was no interface on the inside to interact with, and the metal looked strange. It was pockmarked with countless dents and dimples. Some were the size of a grain of sand, while others were the size of her fist. It made the exterior of the egg-shaped object look weather-beaten and old—really old. In fact, it looked ancient. Whatever it was, it was much older than she was. Adel was only eleven, after all. She glanced behind the object and noticed a very long furrow, hundreds of meters long, that the object had seared into the earth behind it.

Adel instinctively clasped her hand around her necklace. It was a little metal charm in the shape of a pyramid. Her mother had given it to her and it was the most precious thing she owned. She looked down at her arms and legs and realized she was wearing a silver bodysuit with matching moccasin-like shoes seamlessly attached. The outfit was sleeveless, and it had a high collar that stopped just below her jawline. It wasn't the type of clothing she normally wore. She reached up to fix her hair but quickly pulled her hand back in horror. She found she had no hair. She cautiously felt her head—it had been shaved completely smooth.

She forced back tears as it occurred to her that she didn't know where she was, or how she had gotten into that thing—whatever it was. Her entire body felt sore, her mind drifting about in a thick fog. Adel looked around and saw only black earth and a few trees in the distance. Wherever she was, the temperature was warm and she felt light on her feet, although the air was a bit thin. Though she had just woken up, she felt tired for some reason. She sat down cross-legged under the shade of the ancient metal egg.

As she sat there, she closed her eyes and tried to think back, to remember. Her mind was in such a haze, she struggled to remember anything, but eventually flashes of what happened slowly came back to her. She remembered her apartment on Mars with her mother. It had a window, which was useless because it was always dark outside—the sun was just a white speck that grew smaller with each passing day. Adel remembered always being hungry and cold—she was always so cold. Her mom was always away working, or at least that's what she told her. Then, one morning, her mom told her that a ship had come to save the children. To take them to a mothership in space. She asked if her mom could come with. Her mom told her it had room only for children, not for grown-ups. She remembered how she cried and argued when her mother told her she'd have to go alone. She refused to go. Her mom cried that day, and her mom never cried. Adel remembered how her mom sat there with her on the bed for hours. Then her mom gave her some hot chocolate to drink. Chocolate was a very rare treat, and she'd never been given hot chocolate at bedtime. Then she fell asleep . . . and woke up—here. In fact, it had happened only yesterday. She was sure of that.

Adel pulled her legs up to her chest and wrapped her arms around them and sobbed. Her mom had tricked her. Her mom had sent her away even though she didn't want to leave. She didn't care if the sun was dying. She wanted to stay home.

Now, worst of all, she didn't know where she was. It certainly wasn't Mars or Earth. The color of the sky was different. It wasn't blue like Earth or pink like Mars. The sky was a bright magenta. The trees and plants looked peculiar, and the star above had a strange tinge to it that she could only describe as being slightly off from the videos she had seen of the Earth sun. She had wished she had a chance to see it in its former glory for herself, to feel its warmth, and to visit all the exciting places on Earth. A place she had never been to, but the sun was already a mere glimmer of what it once was by the time she was born. As for Earth, her mother said it had become a very scary place.

The planet's sun reached its apex, and she felt herself grow hot. Being too hot was a sensation she had never experienced before. She was thirsty and starting to get hungry as well. She looked inside the metal egg, which she realized was a spacecraft, and found no supplies of any kind. The inside of the craft was still very cold. Adel wandered up a hill toward the tree line. She wasn't sure exactly what she was looking for, but she knew she couldn't just sit there forever. Climbing the hill proved exhausting, and her muscles ached terribly. Her lungs burned for oxygen, and on top of it all, she had a searing headache.

After she reached the top of the hill, she saw a marvelous sight. It was a massive pyramid. It looked similar to the pyramids in

Egypt. She had never seen the real ones in person though she had explored them virtually. It was a dark-gray iridescent metal, just like the charm on her necklace. Before the pyramid was a small city in the middle of a big lake with teal-colored water. It was so clear that even from her vantage point she could see the glimmer of pebbles at the bottom. Causeways connected the city to the surrounding land, and the pyramid stood beyond the lake in the distance. Enveloping the city was lush prairie dotted with cottages and trees. Adel wanted to run toward it, but her legs wouldn't cooperate. They were too stiff and sore. It was as if she hadn't walked in quite some time. Of course, she thought that was silly. She had left only yesterday.

Adel crossed the causeway and reached the outskirts of the city. She noticed there were low walls made of boulders that divided the landscape into rectangles. It looked similar to the way the boundaries of English farms were divided up, only there were no crops, just wild grain wafting in the wind. The stone walls were crumbling as if no one had fixed them for ages. She knocked on the door of the first cottage. The house was made of brick and had a terra-cotta tile roof. Many of the shingles were hanging off, and the roof had a thick cover of weeds growing out of it. The door and the window shutters were closed and made of the same iridescent metal as the pyramid beyond. Even though she was quite sure she was on a different planet, it all looked very familiar and was somehow comforting.

She knocked again and pressed the metal buzzer several times. There was no answer. She walked a little farther and knocked on the door of the next house. No answer. As Adel continued down a narrow road, the buildings became more dense and she found herself in the city proper. Weeds grew out of the pavers, but she could make out a repeating starburst design. There were no people on the streets, and all the shutters and doors were sealed shut. The vine-covered buildings were sturdy but looked old, very old. She got to the town center. It was a perfect circle lined with columns that held up a veranda sheathed with terra-cotta shingles. The top of which looked as if it hadn't been given any attention in a very long time, as it too was overgrown with weeds. Between the columns were statues of men and women and various animals. All of them made of the same peculiar iridescent metal. In the center of the square was a small stone pyramid. Nature seemed to be consuming the entire city: every surface, except the metallic ones, was covered in green.

"Hello. Hello," she called out.

No one answered.

She knocked on the doors of all the shops, but there was no answer. The entire place was deserted. She followed one of the main canals to the far end of the small city, where it met the teal lake. She pressed a circle marked with a dotted line next to her collar bone. "Shoes off," she said. Her shoes parted and folded neatly up her calves like origami. She hung her legs over the edge and put them in the water. It was warm. Adel had never felt water between her toes before. She had watched old movies of people on the beach and played around in virtual beaches, but it wasn't something she was ever able to experience in real life. She peered down and saw schools of fish swimming below. There were no boats or indications of other people.

Adel continued to wander the city. Every street was devoid of life. There weren't even any cats or dogs. Though she did see some birds. They were unlike any bird she had seen before. They had purple and white feathers, their wings had hands in the middle, like a bat, and their rounded beaks had teeth. Adel wasn't sure if they were aliens or dinosaurs, or some genetic experiment. Whatever they were, they were beautiful—in their own way. Every few blocks there was a small park. She walked into one of the parks and noticed a fountain in the middle, again made of the same metal, but there was no water inside. Instead, it was full of branches and leaves, nests of the strange birds. She saw the drooping branches of the trees. They were heavy with fruit. It was a curious type of citrus that had a skin with alternating stripes of red and purple. She snapped one from the branch and peeled the skin away. The inside was a light red. She bit into one of the segments. Sweet juice filled her mouth. It tasted incredible.

After she had gotten her fill of fruit, she sat down under the tree. She had noticed most of the trees and plant life around the city were fruit-bearing, and she recognized several of the other plants as various vegetables and medicinal herbs. In fact, there were so many plants, she suspected they could easily feed the entire city on forage alone. As the sun began to set, the temperature remained warm and seemed to embrace her like a blanket. As her eyelids got heavy, she lay down on a thick bed of wild wheat stalks.

She awoke to the new sun shining on her face. Her headache had gone away, and her body didn't feel as sore as it had the day before. There was another tree that grew blue banana, and she helped herself to a few. She wandered the little park and found some water collected in fleshy scoop-shaped leaves. She knelt down and sucked it up. It tasted fresh and earthy.

It didn't take long for Adel to see most of the city. Its architecture reminded her of Venice, while its layout resembled Tenochtitlan, given its causeways and the way it was placed on an island within a lake. She decided she needed to visit the pyramid.

Adel walked down a long, narrow causeway made of stone. It looked like a Parisian bridge with its many arches made of white stone and its alternating metal statues or lampposts. With each step the pyramid became larger and loomed high over the lush landscape. She passed through a stone edifice with giant columns before eventually reaching the pyramid itself. There were two large double doors. Adel looked around and saw a depression in the form of a human hand. Not knowing what else to do, she pressed her hand against it. She shuddered as the double doors began to creak open. A thick, cold fog emanated toward her. It was pitch-black inside. Adel took several steps back.

She stood there contemplating whether she really wanted to go inside. What would she find in there, and why would a seemingly modern people build such a thing? Then again, it occurred to her that they might not have been people. Adel held out her hands—the air felt very cold. She hated the cold. She rubbed her bare arms and then pushed the circle next to her collar bone. "Sleeves," she said. Fabric unfolded in a hexagonal pattern down her arms and stopped when it had looped around her thumbs. She looked at her arms, satisfied, and pressed the circle again. "Hood." The fabric gave a slight glow as a hood unfurled behind her neck. She reached behind her and pulled it up over her bald head. She gritted her teeth as she pondered stepping forward.

Adel took a deep breath and walked into the pyramid. It was dark, like the inside of her spacecraft. She was about to turn around, but then the ground before her lit up with a clear white light. As she moved, lights turned on along the interior walls of the pyramid. There were no floors. It was just one massive interior space. There was a mechanical squeaking and crashing sound above her. Dust and clods of dirt fell from the hole above and into the chamber in which she stood. She could see the magenta sky as the top of the pyramid opened slightly. Then a single white light in the center of the pyramid speared upward out of the floor and into the heavens. Adel could feel her pulse racing, and part of her wanted to run away, but still she found herself walking toward it. She thought she heard footsteps behind her. She stopped and listened. Nothing.

It was the most perfect light she had ever seen. It was the only way she could describe it. Entranced, she held out her hand, wanting to touch it. Her hand reached toward the light, and then she had second thoughts and pulled it back. There was a shuffling sound behind her. Adel turned her head sharply, but there was only emptiness. She sat down cross-legged and put her face in her hands, struggling to hold back another onset of tears. She felt so alone.

Adel climbed to her feet and turned to leave. She thought the structure was the most useless waste of resources she had ever seen. As she reached the doorway, she heard footsteps behind her again. She stopped, and the footsteps behind her did too. She slowly turned. Her mouth hung open and her blood froze. A smiling man was standing before her. He wore spotless white flowing robes. He was an adult, maybe twenty-five years old, and his features were unusual. Everything about his face was symmetrical and formed in a way that could only be described as perfect.

"Good morning, Adel," he said.

Adel blinked hard. Her vision was fuzzy. She realized she was on the floor and the man was standing over her. She had fainted. Adel figured the stress was getting to her. She stood and brushed herself off.

"How do you know my name?"

"We've been waiting for you."

"Why?"

"So that you can safely reach this place. I am the conductor, and I have been following you for a very long time."

Adel walked in nervous circles around the conductor. He simply stood there with his hands in front of him with his fingers and thumbs touching to make a sort of inverted triangle shape. She noticed that the dust in the air above seemed to be floating through him.

"Are you a hologram?" she asked.

"No," he replied.

"An alien?"

The man smiled. "No."

Adel reached under her hood and scratched her bald head.

131

She saw that the man didn't leave any footprints in the fine mist of dust that had collected on the floor.

"Are you a ghost?"

"No, Adel, I was like you once, and now I am the conductor. Please have a seat."

The gray-colored metal beneath her feet glowed with a rainbow of iridescence. Tiny particles materialized from the floor and created a seat behind her. She cautiously sat down. The seat fit her body perfectly, and though it was metal, or whatever the material was, it was warm to the touch and comfortable.

There was a long silence. Adel opened her mouth to speak, but the man, as if reading her thoughts, spoke first. He explained that what he was going to tell her would be difficult to hear and if she didn't want to hear it, she could wait, but he advised her not to wait too long. Adel thought about that carefully and decided that whatever it was, no matter how ugly, she needed to know. She figured he was going to tell her that her mother had died. Of course, she already knew that. They both knew they were going to die, for years. What surprised her was that she had somehow lived. He asked her again, this time more slowly, if she wanted to know the truth. Adel nodded.

"Adel, how old do you think you are?"

"I'm eleven Earth years old. I turned eleven a few days before, before my mom put me to sleep."

There was another long pause as the conductor walked slowly around her with his hands still held before him in their unusual triangular position.

"That's true—in a sense. You are biologically eleven Earth years old. But chronologically you are 39,782 Earth years old."

She shook her head in disbelief as her eyes welled up. That was impossible, people couldn't live that long. Why would he make up such a terrible lie?

"You're lying. You're trying to trick me."

"I have no reason to lie. As you might have figured out already, you were put in permanent stasis, a state in which an organism can remain indefinitely, so long as the organism is protected within the confines of its chamber."

"No, that's not possible, and even if it was—ships can't last that long."

"There are no moving parts in your pod, and permanent stasis requires no maintenance so long as the environment around the organism is not disturbed."

Adel wanted to argue, screaming and yelling at this man, but she found herself choking up, drowning within her own tears. She slid out of the chair and fell to her knees in despair.

She must have cried for a couple of hours while the conductor patiently, quietly waited. Adel wiped her face with the back of her hand and climbed to her feet.

"I want to know why I'm here," she asked.

"You may want to sit back down."

"No. Tell me. Tell me now."

The conductor gave a gentle nod and motioned for her to look upward. The entire inside of the pyramid lit up with holograms. She saw a massive mothership crossing the galaxy. It was adjacent to a bright blue gas giant of a planet. It had millions of pods like hers attached to the outer hull. There was a flash of light. Her heart shuddered. A meteor hit the mothership. The pods and the ship disappeared into the ethereal atmosphere of the planet. A few pods remained, floating about in the asteroid belt until, one by one, they each collided with the massive chunks of ice and rock or got sucked down into the planet. But one pod, just one out of millions, floated off into a different direction, propelled away to safety by the very impact that destroyed the others. When her pod reached a certain distance, its engines engaged briefly to set a preprogrammed course, and it disappeared into the blackness of space.

Adel was back on the floor again. She was holding her arms and rocking back and forth. She had more questions, but she was afraid to ask them. The conductor was still there, patiently waiting. She pulled her hood over her eyes. She didn't want to look at him or his awful holographic histories. After sitting there for quite some time, Adel decided to speak.

"What is it you really want to say to me?"

"Adel, I know this is difficult, but you are the last one."

"The last one?"

"The last human."

She seemed to have no more tears to shed. Ever since she had set foot on the planet, her world had been torn inside out. She didn't want to believe the conductor, but there was a feeling— an indescribable feeling—deep down inside her that told her every word he said was true.

"How did the people in the city die?" she asked.

"Most of them didn't die."

Adel's eyes perked up. It wasn't a response she had expected, given the awful information that kept spewing out of the conductor's mouth.

"What happened to them?"

The conductor gave another gentle smile. "They transcended."

"Transcended?"

It took quite some time for the conductor to explain the history that had passed. There were twelve mother ships. Mostly for the better-off citizenry of Earth and Mars. The twelfth ship was destroyed in a disaster, but the eleventh ship came back for the children. It was designed differently from the others. It was a completely automated ship made just for children. Ten of the ships managed to find planets on which to settle and eventually grow colonies. The people on the other colonies modified themselves to such an extent with genetics and cybernetics that they were no longer human—they became something else, or were destroyed by their creations. These beings that used to be human even learned to travel the universe without the use of archaic spacecraft. They were in stark contrast to the people on the planet where she was now, who were considered extremist holdouts clinging to a primitive and backward existence. However, even the last holdouts couldn't resist the urge to change eventually. After all, the locals named the planet Transcendence.

The hologram around her showed what life was once like on Transcendence. Everyone was permanently young. Most didn't allow themselves to age more than twenty-five biological Earth years, yet most were in actuality several thousand years old. Human depopulation was an issue for the planet. There were very few children because people didn't feel the need to keep reproducing once their families had become a certain size. And people rarely died. Stopping and even reversing aging was something scientists had cracked before Adel was born, but it wasn't common in her time because of the turmoil. But the people of this planet chose to live in small, charming cities, villages, and farms constructed mostly from natural materials. Their technology was such that they didn't have to farm, forage, or cook, or make wine, but they did so anyway. She thought it strange that such an advanced people chose to live deliberately simple and primitive lifestyles. Then they decided to take a leap, to change, and they built the pyramid.

Adel had a sneaking suspicion about the conductor. She stood and walked up to the man, and when she tried to touch him, her hand went right through him. For his part, the conductor was completely unfazed by it. She gazed up at the spear of light in the center of the pyramid before turning back toward the conductor.

"You're not human, are you?"

"Not anymore. I'm a representation that was deemed familiar to you."

"Because you transcended?"

"Yes."

"What is transcendence?"

The conductor explained how, at first, people were content to simply modify their genes to improve themselves. They lengthened their lives, improved their intelligence, and removed their worst tendencies. But it only took them so far because—initially—they wanted to remain human. Then they had a change of heart and invented something. Something that would free them of the confines of their organic bodies to become one with the universe, with everything. With other life-forms, the stars, to enter the spaces between spaces and gain a level of sentience and intelligence simply not possible for an organic or cybernetic creature, no matter how far evolved.

A metal relief with a hand imprint materialized in front of the beam of light. Adel looked at it. Then she looked at her own hand. It was a perfect match. The conductor gestured for her to press her palm on top of it. Adel held her hand over the interface, but then pulled it back.

"You don't have to be alone, Adel."

"What if I don't want to transcend? What if I want to stay human?"

"That is your choice. Many others chose not to transcend. They lived quite some time and then they eventually passed on. Interestingly, death was a decision usually made by choice. The last of them chose to die nine hundred years ago. But if you're frightened, we can allow you to experience transcendence temporarily before you make your decision."

After several minutes of pacing, Adel decided to try temporary transcendence. She slowly lowered her hand on the interface and stepped into the beam of light. She felt a sensation of overwhelming cold followed by equally overwhelming heat. Then she experienced an almost omniscient sentience. She could feel the pulse of other living things, trillions of them, all at once, and she could feel the fabric of the cosmos itself. There was no time in the realm she found herself in. She was everywhere and nowhere all at once. Past, present, and future existed together in a single looped continuum. She could see her mom and all kinds of people from ages past.

Adel seemed to feel every emotion she was capable of all at

once. She drifted through a seemingly infinite number of different times and places. Then she came upon a single event out of countless events within space-time. Oddly, that single event, out of the infinity of events, pulled her toward it like no other. There was a young woman, from an ancient time, near a stream. The Neanderthal woman wore furs and had a baby on her back. Adel could sense events that had already happened and hadn't happened all at the same time, and which had occurred in an infinite number of ways. The young woman was her ancestor, and she too would lose her parents, and like Adel she was also the last of her kind. Adel could sense that the woman was about to go back to her dwelling and be killed and consumed in nearly every parallel instance. Adel snapped off her necklace with the little pyramid charm and dropped it. It splashed loudly into the stream behind the woman. She turned and picked up the charm from the water. Then she stopped. The young woman sat down and made a necklace out of it rather than head back to her dwelling right away. It bought the woman some time and changed her timeline. Instead of getting killed, she would now live. Adel felt the effect ripple across countless dimensions, and in an instant the light was gone.

Adel was back in the pyramid. The conductor was watching her. She reached around her neck to find her charm gone. It was real. It was all real. The sensation could only be described as incredible. For a moment she had felt big, and now she felt small and insignificant.

"So, Adel, do you wish to transcend?"

Adel thought about it and then shook her head. "No."

"No? You are indeed rare. Almost everyone who experiences transcendence chooses to go through with it."

"I want to live in a cottage next to the city. Can I do that?"

"I'll open the doors and provide you with everything you require to start your life here, if that is your wish."

Adel remembered everything she had experienced and the countless lives she had managed to live through in the mere nanoseconds she had experienced transcendence. Her knowledge and intelligence had easily grown ten thousand-fold within that time—limited only by the confines of her simple human brain. She was human, a fragile and primitive creature, but it was an existence she accepted. Adel turned toward the conductor.

"I don't want to be alone."

The conductor held his hand out toward the light. "Then transcend."

"No. I want someone to live with me and share my life with."

"You're the last one, Adel. There are no others."

"But you can make one, here within the pyramid. You have the genetic information of my people stored within and the means to create living organisms—like people."

The conductor said the pyramid could do no such thing for it was against the ethics of the people who built the pyramid. They didn't think it was proper to create human life from scratch, so they programmed the pyramid with an ethic protocol to forbid it from ever doing so.

"I'm the last human, so I can order the pyramid to change the rules," she said.

The conductor shook his head. He said changing the rules required a quorum of nine, and she was only one. As Adel's eyes began to well up, the conductor held up his forefinger and said there was an exception. The pyramid's programming would allow only twenty-three chromosomes, half of the required forty-six, to be transferred from the vault to make life. A living person was required to provide the other twenty-three. He said that she could come back to the pyramid after she had become a woman, and if she so chose, the pyramid would unlock its genetic vaults and transfer those twenty-three chromosomes to her, granting her a child, and that she could come back, as often as she chose, should she want more children.

Adel walked out of the pyramid. It was warm outside. She closed her eyes and took in the fresh air. It was a bit thin, but she knew she'd get used to it. She found a small farmhouse with its metal door open. As the conductor promised, an abundance of supplies had been generated inside for her.

There were blankets, food, water, and a little box that contained a large variety of seeds. There was also a sundress neatly folded on her bed. She changed out of her bodysuit and put on the flowing yellow garment. It felt soft against her skin and was much more comfortable. She stepped outside and found a hand plow leaning against the farmhouse—made of the same peculiar metal as her charm. Though the plow hadn't been touched in ages, the blade was still sharp. She removed it from its resting place, wandered out to the grass-strewn field, and began to turn the hard soil.

AΩ